MENSA
WHODUNITS

Bill Wise, Hy Conrad & Bob Peterson

OFFICIAL MENSA
PUZZLE BOOK

Main Street
A division of Sterling Publishing Co., Inc.
New York

Library of Congress Cataloging-in-Publication Data Available

2 4 6 8 10 9 7 5 3 1

This book is excerpted from the following Sterling titles:
Detective Club Puzzlers: Solve-It-Yourself Mysteries
© 1997 by Hy Conrad & Bob Peterson
Illustrations © 1997 by Lucy Corvino
Whodunit Crime Puzzles by Hy Conrad,
© 2002 by Hy Conrad & Tatjana Mai Wyss
Whodunit Math Puzzles © 2002 by Bill Wise

Published by Sterling Publishing Co., Inc.
387 Park Avenue South, New York, NY 10016
© 2004 by Sterling Publishing Co., Inc.
Distributed in Canada by Sterling Publishing
c/o Canadian Manda Group, One Atlantic Avenue, Suite 105
Toronto, Ontario, Canada M6K 3E7
Distributed in Great Britain and Europe by Chris Lloyd at Orca Book
Services, Stanley House, Fleets Lane, Poole BH15 3AJ, England
Distributed in Australia by Capricorn Link (Australia) Pty. Ltd.
P.O. Box 704, Windsor, NSW 2756, Australia

Printed in United States of America

ISBN 1-4027-1643-5

CONTENTS

THE CRIME SOLVER'S HANDBOOK

A Basic Reference Manual for Detectives in the Field

Codes

Criminals and spies may use secret codes in order to
disguise their messages.

There are two main types of code. One is a
transposition code. That's where all the right letters are
there in the message, just mixed up. The easiest
transposition code is simply writing the message
backwards. If a secret message contains a lot of
unusual letters, a lot of Q's, for example, then it's probably not a transposition code.

The second basic type is a *substitution code*, in which
every letter in the message is a substitute for the real
letter. In order to crack a substitution code, you have
to go through the message carefully, substituting letters
by trial and error until the words start making sense.

Here are some tips for solving substitution codes.

- The most often used letter in the English language is
  E, followed by T, A, 0, and N. Find the most used
  letter in your message and try substituting an E for it.
- The most common letter beginning a word is T.
- The most common letter at the end of a word is E.
- A one-letter word is almost always A or I.

- The most common two-letter words are OF, TO, and IN.
- The most common three-letter words are THE and AND. The most common four-letter word is THAT.
- Q is always followed by U.
- See any double letters? The most common double letters are LL, followed by EE, SS, OO, and TT.

Invisible Ink

Any citrus juice—lemon, orange, lime, or grapefruit—can be used to make invisible ink. Onion juice also works. To write a message in invisible ink, use a small brush rather than a stick or fountain pen. A stick or pen can leave pressure marks. After writing your message with the juice, be sure to let it dry properly.

To recover an invisible message, heat the paper slowly over a hot light bulb. The message will turn brown. Be careful not to singe the paper with the bulb. *Never use fire.*

Sending Messages with Mirrors

To send a mirror message, you must keep two things in
mind, your *light source* and your *target*, the person you
want to receive the message. In most cases, you will
want to use the sun as your source. If the sun isn't

shining, or if it's night, a nearby lamp will also work.

Take a small mirror. Face it directly toward the light source. From this position, slowly tilt the mirror until it's facing halfway between the light source and your target. If the sun is bright, a flash of light will land on your target. Practice tilting the mirror back and forth until you can make a long or short flash of light whenever you want. If you're using a lamp or the sun is not bright, don't worry. Your target will be able to see the flash even if you can't. It just takes more practice on your part to line up the mirror.

Try it with a partner. Use Morse code. Or make up your own simple code, such as *four flashes* means "Come quickly."

Write out what you want to send ahead of time and ask your partner to write down what he or she receives. Work on accuracy. With a little practice, you will be able to send almost any message using nothing more than a small mirror.

International Morse Code

This is the most commonly used code in the world. After flashing each letter, pause slightly. When receiving a message in Morse code, write down the dots and dashes. You'll have plenty of time later to translate them into letters.

A • –	M – –	Y – • – –
B – • • •	N – •	Z – – • •
C – • – •	O – – –	1 • – – – –
D – • •	P • – – •	2 • • – – –
E •	Q – – • –	3 • • • – –
F • • – •	R • – •	4 • • • • –
G – – •	S • • •	5 • • • • •
H • • • •	T –	6 – • • • •
I • •	U • • –	7 – – • • •
J • – – –	V • • • –	8 – – – • •
K – • –	W • – –	9 – – – – •
L • – • •	X – • • –	0 – – – – –

Disappearing Ink

Disappearing ink can be easily made from three ingredients: water, iodine, and starch. Iodine can be bought from a drugstore, while all-purpose cooking starch is easily found in most grocery stores. Combine equal parts water, iodine, and starch. Mix well; otherwise the starch will not properly dissolve and will leave a grainy residue. The finished mixture will resemble a blue-black ink.

Disappearing ink can be applied with a narrow-tip brush or with a refillable fountain pen. If using a fountain pen, try not to write with too much pressure. Excess pressure will result in pressure lines on the paper. In about three days, the ink will completely disappear.

Dusting for Fingerprints

Take a clean fingerprint brush. A make-up brush will also do. Roll the brush handle between your hands to separate the bristles. Now inspect the surface to be dusted at different angles of light. This may make a latent print visible to the eye.

Dip the brush lightly into fingerprint powder, barely touching the powder. Apply a dusting of powder to the surface using light, even strokes. Any smudge that appears may prove to be a print. To clean the print, gently brush it, being sure to go with the flow of the ridges. Gently blowing on the print can also remove excess powder.

Now take a roll of fingerprint tape. Transparent tape can also be used. Pull out enough tape to cover the area (usually 5 to 6 inches), holding the roll firmly in one hand and the tape end in the other. Secure the tape to the area above the print; then slide your thumb along the tape, forcing it down gently over the print. Hold the roll tightly in the other hand. Carefully, smooth down the tape over the print, forcing out all the air bubbles. The print is now protected.

To lift the print, slowly pull up the roll end of the tape until the entire tape is removed. Attach the taped print to a fingerprint card, again being sure to smooth out all air bubbles. Cut off the excess tape and promptly label the fingerprint card with the exact location, date, and time of the procedure.

Fingerprints can be easily lifted from any hard, smooth surface. Glass, metal, and hard plastic are good places to look for prints.

Identifying Prints

No two people have the same fingerprints. And each finger on a person's hand is different from the others. You and everyone else in the world have ten unique prints. This makes it very important to distinguish which finger you are trying to match. The prints found most often are from the index and middle fingers of the right hand. Thumbprints are the easiest prints to identify. Look at your own hand. At the top of your right thumb, you will notice that the ridges flow up and away from the fingers. The same is true for your left thumb.

Fingerprint patterns can be divided into arches (plain arches and tented arches), loops (radial loops and ulnar loops), and whorls (plain whorls, double loop whorls, central pocket loop whorls, and accidental whorls). This makes eight basic patterns. Sixty percent of all prints are loops, while 35 percent are whorls.

First look at the print you need to match. Identify which of the eight patterns it falls into (see diagram).

Once you establish this, you can proceed. If a suspect's print does not match this basic pattern, you can eliminate him.

If a suspect's print does match your print's basic pattern, the job of elimination becomes harder. You must now look for identification points.

Compare the unique identification points of the suspect's prints with the same areas of the print you need to match. Even one point of difference between prints can eliminate that suspect.

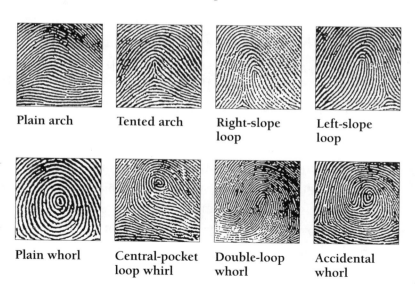

Plain arch   **Tented arch**   **Right-slope loop**   **Left-slope loop**

Plain whorl   **Central-pocket loop whirl**   **Double-loop whorl**   **Accidental whorl**

Elimination Fingerprints

Elimination prints are taken directly from a subject's hands and are kept on file for future reference. To take elimination prints, you need an ink pad and a card with room for ten fingerprints and notations.

Have the subject wash his hands. Then take him by the wrist, instructing him to relax his hand and arm muscles. Roll the left thumb on the ink pad, making sure to roll it toward his body. Be sure to hold the four fingers back so they are not accidentally inked. Immediately repeat this rolling process on the proper space on the print card. Repeat this with the four fingers of the left hand. In the case of fingers, roll them away from the subject's body, not toward it. Do the same with the right hand, thumb first, then fingers.

Many police departments also record palm prints. To take a palm print, ink the subject's entire palm and all his fingers.

Then press the entire hand straight down on a card. Use a different card for each hand.

If an ink pad is not available, elimination prints can be taken the same way as latent prints. Have the subject roll each clean finger onto a card. Allow the card to dry for a few minutes. Then dust the prints with fingerprint powder and protect with fingerprint tape.

Hair and Fiber Analysis

Everywhere we go, we leave behind hairs from our bodies and fibers from our clothing. At a crime scene, the police gather these small pieces of evidence, often with the help of special vacuum cleaners, in the hope of determining who has been on the scene.

Even with the most advanced equipment, the police can rarely say positively that a hair or fiber came from a specific person. However, even without advanced equipment, you can still make a few deductions through careful examination.

First, is your sample a hair or fiber? Examine it with a magnifying glass. A hair gets narrower from the shaft to the tip. Hairs also have different textures from fibers. Examine several human hairs from different sources. Place each hair against a white background. You'll quickly be able to determine color, texture, curliness, length, maybe even dandruff or other characteristics. Using this evidence, you won't be able to make a positive identification, but you will be able to narrow down your field of suspects.

Treat fibers the same way. Again, you will not be able to state positively that the fiber you're examining came from a certain sweater or blanket. But you will be able to narrow down the field and maybe make a few reasonable deductions about who has been on the scene.

Blood Evidence

NEVER EXPERIMENT WITH BLOOD: NOT WITH YOUR OWN BLOOD—NOT WITH ANYONE ELSE'S.

Investigators can learn a great deal from blood, starting with the species of animal.

If the blood sample is human, then investigators can test DNA (deoxyribonucleic acid). DNA is the basic chromosome pattern that makes you look the way you do. Every person in the world has a different DNA pattern. By testing blood for DNA, police can identify the person that a drop of blood came from, sometimes with 99.99 percent accuracy.

Due to scientific advances, more and more can be discovered from blood all the time. Police are now able to determine the things listed on the following page.

- the position of persons or objects at the crime scene at the time of the attack
- the distance the blood fell and at what speed
- whether the blow was from a sharp or blunt instrument
- the number of blows
- the movements of people at the scene after the attack
- the time between the attack and the examination
- whether a bloody wound occurred prior to a fall or as the result of a fall

Even if a perpetrator has wiped blood away, investigators can still see it by the use of Luminol, a chemical spray. After an area has been sprayed with Luminol, a fluorescent lamp will show traces of blood that would otherwise be invisible to the naked eye.

It's also important to note that bloodstains are not always red. Especially when dry, blood can appear black, green, blue, even grayish-white.

By examining the shape of a bloodstain (the blood spatter pattern), a great deal can be learned about a crime. For instance, a small, thick stain indicates that the blood fell a short distance. A larger, thinner stain means it fell from a greater height.

If blood falls straight down from a wound, the spatter pattern will be more or less symmetrical. If the drop looks like a bowling pin or an exclamation point, it means that the body was moving at the time it was bleeding. The smaller end of the drop points in the direction the bleeder was moving.

Fake Blood

If you wish to experiment with fake blood spatters, make up a batch of fake blood. You can do this by combining water, red food coloring, a drop of blue food coloring, and a dash of corn syrup to thicken it. By using an eyedropper, you can reproduce various blood spatter patterns and examine them.

CAUTION: Food coloring can stain many surfaces. Do *not* use this mixture on clothing.

Lie-Detecting Methods

There is no such thing as a foolproof lie detector. The polygraph machines used by police measure a suspect's pulse rate, breathing, and blood pressure. When these increase suddenly, the police assume that the person is more nervous and, therefore, lying.

But you don't need a polygraph machine to detect a case of nerves. These cues can also indicate nervousness and possible lying.

- dry mouth and sweaty palms
- refusing to make eye contact with the questioner
- distracted eye movements
- nervous twitches
- a suddenly slower speech pattern
- stammering or pausing significantly between statements
- habitually answering a question with a question
- trying to distract the questioner or change subjects

A favorite police technique is to rephrase the same question over and over in the hope that the suspect will trip himself up in a contradiction.

Crime-Scene Sketches

While photographs of a scene are an essential part of a criminal investigation, they cannot replace a good crime-scene sketch. Both photographs and sketches are important. A photograph records everything, even details overlooked by the detective. A well-done sketch, on the other hand, will show only the most important elements and can often help a detective better think through a situation after he leaves the scene. Also, a sketch can better reveal measurements and the relationships between objects.

You do not need artistic skill to draw a usable crime scene sketch. These tips should help.

• Your first sketch, done at the scene, can be rough. Don't worry about straight lines and neatness. Just get the measurements and details right. Later, using tools like a ruler, protractor, and compass, you can draw the finished sketch.

• Include the major items of physical evidence and where you found them. Measure distances as accurately as possible.

- Be consistent. If you are using a tape measure, use a tape measure for *all* your measurements. If you are pacing off distances, then pace off *all* distances.

- Include all critical features of the room or outdoor scene.

- Make the sketch easy to understand. Do not include too much detail.

- Label the sketch with your name, the date, the time, and the location. If you are using symbols or abbreviations in the sketch, include a legend that explains them.

When drawing a crucial object, such as a corpse, use the triangulation method to establish the exact location. This is done by measuring the distance to it from at least two widely separated locations.

How to Tail a Suspect

In order to find out more about a person's habits and acquaintances, it is often necessary to tail your suspect. The primary goals of a tail are (a) not losing track of your suspect and (b) not allowing him to discover the tail. Here are some hints for tailing a suspect.

- **Stay a safe distance back.** Remain as far back as you can while still keeping your suspect in sight. Half to one block is usually sufficient. In most cases, it's better to lose a tail than to let your suspect know he's being followed.

- **Be inconspicuous.** Try to blend in. Avoid quick movements. Don't draw attention to yourself by dressing out of place or wearing a wild disguise. If the suspect knows you, try wearing clothes of yours he hasn't seen. Something as simple as a different cap and dark glasses can change your appearance from a distance.

- **Use reflective surfaces.** If you have to get close to your suspect, avoid looking directly at him. Instead, use reflective surfaces, such as a store or car window, to keep an eye on his movements.

- **Be aware of peripheral vision.** In many cases, a suspect will be able to see you without looking directly at you. This is called *peripheral vision*. Even if you're off to one side, your suspect may be able to see you out of the corner of his eye.

- **Practice.** Try practicing with a friend. Tail him without letting him know you're there. See how long you can do it without being discovered. See how closely you can tail him before he sees you. This will teach you how far you have to stay behind a real suspect.

Footprint Evidence

Footprint evidence can be an important part of an investigation. Even in the best of circumstances, however, it doesn't give the detective a great amount of information.

Athletic shoes have the easiest soles to match. If you are working with a clear print of an athletic shoe, you can usually determine the shoe's brand, model, and size. If you see no wear or variation in the pattern, then the shoe that made the impression is probably fairly new. If there is a distinctive wear pattern in the impression, however, you will have a better chance of matching your print to a particular suspect's shoe.

Photograph a footprint before you take a plaster cast of it. Carefully remove twigs, leaves, or other debris. A ruler should be placed directly above or below the footprint to indicate scale. If any mistakes happen during the casting process, you will have the photograph as evidence.

Before taking a cast, make sure the print is not overly wet. If you cannot wait for the natural drying process to occur, use a heat source, such as a portable hair dryer. Make sure not to bring the heat too close to the print. Do not let the dryer blow directly on the print since this may damage it. And don't let the print become too dry. This will cause flaking and will damage the print. It should be just dry enough to hold the plaster of Paris.

Set up a metal frame around the entire print, pressing it gently into the soil. This will keep the print from expanding or changing shape during the casting process.

Mix plaster of Paris according to the directions on the box. Be aware, plaster hardens fairly quickly. Use a rubber mixing bowl if you can, since plaster will not stick to rubber. If no rubber bowl is available, use any clean bowl that can be thrown out afterward.

Start with the amount of water you think would comfortably fill the footprint impression. Add plaster and mix, continuing to add plaster until the mixture has the thickness of pancake batter.

Pour the plaster continuously, starting from one end of the footprint and working toward the other. This will help avoid air bubbles. Do not pour the mixture directly from the bowl into the impression. This can damage it. Always use a spoon or spatula to break the plaster's fall. The overall thickness of the finished cast should be 1 to 1½ inches (about 2.5 to 4 cm).

After pouring in the mixture, reinforce the cast. The best material to use is wire screening, cut into 2-by-4-inch (5- by 10-cm) strips. Imbed these in the wet plaster. This will help prevent the cast from breaking when you remove it. If you do not have wire screening, green twigs can be used instead.

In 30 minutes the cast should be hard. Remove the metal frame, then lift the cast, being careful not to bend it. After the cast dries for another 30 minutes, use a soft-bristle brush to remove any soil clinging to the bottom.

Now you can compare your finished cast with the soles of your suspect's shoes.

SOLVE-IT-YOURSELF
MYSTERIES

INTRODUCTION

Greg Rydell and Carrie Ingram are best friends, and they love to play detectives, real detectives, who use genuine police methods to solve real crimes. That's why they formed the Detective Club, so that they could investigate all the mysteries that pop up around their suburban Washington, D.C., neighborhood.

To solve their first case, Carrie borrows a book from her father, a police officer. *The Crime Solver's Handbook* teaches them techniques for taking fingerprints, analyzing blood spatters, tailing a suspect, and more. These methods are useful when the young detectives dive into a summer that's full of cases: a simple jewelry theft, a con game, and even an actual murder.

Solve-It-Yourself Mysteries follows Greg and Carrie through three adventures and seven solve-it-yourself crime stories. After reading each story, it's up to you to solve the mystery, then to look up the solution.

If you want to play detective yourself, investigating mysteries around your own neighborhood, look through *The Crime Solver's Handbook* at the beginning of the book. It gives you instructions on how to do everything from tailing suspects to making footprint casts.

Maybe you can be as good a detective as Greg and Carrie. Let's find out.

FINGERPRINTING FOOLS

There it was, lying in the box on top of an old book and a red shawl. Carrie couldn't resist. She picked up the gold brooch, then walked over to the bedroom's full-length mirror.

"Trying on Aunt Mimi's jewelry?"

Carrie turned with a start and saw Greg's mom standing behind her. "Dr. Rydell!" She stammered and blushed and returned the brooch to the cardboard box.

"Pretty, isn't it?" Dr. Rydell said with a smile. "My aunt is so forgetful. She spends one week with us and leaves behind enough to fill a packing crate. Oh, Greg, can you do me a favor?"

Greg had followed his mom into the guest room. "The usual box for Aunt Mimi," he guessed. "You want me to take it to the post office?"

"No hurry," Dr. Rydell said, as she used a roll of clear packing tape to seal the box. "I'd do it myself, but I'm late for the hospital. You remember Aunt Mimi's address?"

Greg nodded. How could he forget the address of his favorite aunt, crazy Aunt Mimi, who made her chauffeur drive around in her own private yellow taxi cab?

An hour later, Greg and Carrie were in the upstairs den, playing the private detective game Greg had gotten last Christmas. Carrie was a full year older than Greg. They lived just three doors from each other and had been best friends ever since they could remember.

"I'm tired of playing," Carrie sighed and put the tiny magnifying glass back in the game box.

"Me, too." Greg's face brightened. "I know. Let's go mail the package."

It was a sunny summer afternoon. They raced down the hall to the guest room and Greg won. That made him the first to see it, an open cardboard box and an empty spot on the red shawl where the brooch used to be.

"It's gone!" he gasped.

Carrie was right behind him. "The brooch!" she yelped. She pushed past him and dove into the box, rummaging through to the bottom. "It's gone!" she echoed in a whisper. "Maybe your mom took it out. Or your sister."

"Mom went right to the hospital As for Becca..."

Greg led the way downstairs where Rebecca and her friend Alicia were on the living room phone and the kitchen extension—talking to boys, of course. Greg

made a point of annoying his older sister, so she wasn't surprised when he interrupted their latest bout of giggling and demanded to know how long they'd been in the house.

"We got here right before your mom went to work," Alicia growled.

"Was anyone else in the house?" Greg asked. Rebecca went back to giggling on the phone. "Becca!"

"Rebecca," she corrected him for the hundredth time. "Urn. Yeah. Eddy next door. He dropped over to get back some video you borrowed from him."

"Did he go upstairs?"

"I don't know. Can't you see we're busy?"

Carrie put on her sweetest smile and tried her own strategy. "Did you see that terrific brooch your Aunt Mimi accidentally left here?"

The older girls looked blankly at each other, then at Carrie.

"It was upstairs in a box in the guest room. Maybe you saw it? Or borrowed it?"

Rebecca shook her head. "The only brooch I ever saw Aunt Mimi wear was some old-fashioned gold thing. No wonder she left it behind."

* * *

"What are you doing?" Greg asked. Carrie had gone home for lunch and Greg hadn't realized she had come back. But here she was again in the guest room, sitting on the floor by Aunt Mimi's box. A small make-up brush was in one hand, a container of black powder in the other.

"Dusting for fingerprints," answered Carrie.

"Cool." Greg plopped down by her side, fascinated.

"You can't tell anyone about the brooch, not until we get it back. Your mom saw me playing with it. She'll think I took it."

"No." Greg thought again. "Well, maybe. I can't believe anyone would just steal Aunt Mimi's pin."

"Well, it didn't disappear."

"Who do you think took it? My sister? Alicia? What about Eddy?"

"They're our three primary suspects," Carrie agreed. "But first, we need evidence."

"Like real detectives." Greg inspected the open cardboard box. "I don't see any prints."

"You can't see most prints until you dust. It's all in there." She pointed to a book propped open on a nearby chair. "*The Crime Solver's Handbook* from Dad's study." Carrie's father was a police detective. On rainy days, the two friends liked to sneak a peek at his old manuals.

Greg looked over Carrie's shoulder. She was dusting a smudge on the sticky side of the clear tape that once held the top flaps in place. "You found a print," he

said, then lost his enthusiasm. "There must be a ton of prints on that box: my mom's, yours."

"Not on the inside of the packing tape," Carrie replied. "I never touched the tape. Your mom touched the ends and the non-sticky side. Remember? This print has to belong to the thief." Carrie finished dusting, then used a pair of scissors to cut out the piece of packing tape with the print on it. She held it up to the light and gazed at the black circular pattern of lines.

"Neat." Greg smiled, then frowned. "I guess we'll need to get fingerprint samples from our suspects. That's going to be hard."

"You don't have to help if you don't want to," said Carrie testily.

"Course I want to. But how do we get their prints? I mean, without them knowing?"

Carrie sighed, as if it were the easiest thing in the world. "We get a suspect to touch a smooth, hard surface. Then we lift the print." She examined the piece of packing tape and compared it to her own thumb. "It's a thumb. A left thumbprint. I know that from the handbook. All we have to do is get our suspects to touch something with their left thumb. Then we dust and lift those prints and compare them to this tape."

"Sounds easy," Greg agreed. "If we're lucky, we'll get that gold pin back in the box before anyone knows the difference."

Carrie removed the old tape from the flaps and

threw it away. Then she took the roll of tape and sealed the box again, making it look just the way it did before the theft.

"Perfect," Greg said. "I'll tell Mom I forgot and that I'll mail it off tomorrow."

Carrie smiled nervously. "Thanks for helping out."

Greg smiled back. "Hey, why not? It's our first real detective case."

* * *

They soon learned how hard being a detective was. They had to actually see the suspect make the print. That was the only way to make sure whose it was. Greg was surprised at how few times people touched hard, shiny surfaces with their left thumbs. It was the next morning before they had their first success.

Greg had found Alicia by the front door, waiting for his sister to come downstairs. "You and Becca going to the mall?" he asked politely.

"What's it to you, dweeb?"

"Oh, nothing. It's just that . . . . You know, I didn't think you'd want to go to the mall. I mean, since you have such a big . . . you know . . . a zit."

"A zit?" Her voice erupted with panic as she turned

to the wall mirror. "Where? Where's the zit?"

"The light's not very good here," Greg said. "There on your left cheek. Don't touch it. That just makes it worse."

Alicia held her face an inch from the glass. "Of all the rotten luck. It must just be starting. I don't see . . ."

"There." Greg pointed. "That red, blotchy dot. Gross!"

"Oh, no!" She had her left cheek nearly plastered against the glass, touching the surface with her left hand. Greg made a mental note of the position of her thumb. Alicia looked and looked. "I don't have a zit!"

"'Course not, Leesh," Rebecca said as she bounced down the stairs. "I would have told you."

"Oooh! Your brother!" Alicia made a move as if to slap him. "Zits are something you don't joke about."

Greg watched the two girls walk out the front door. Then he turned back to the mirror and broke into a grin.

It was Carrie who took care of print number two. As soon as Rebecca came home from the mall, the young detective followed Greg's sister upstairs, pretending to be interested in fingernail care. Ten minutes later, Carrie walked into Greg's room holding the rounded end of a shiny, stainless-steel nail file. "Nice big thumbprint," she proudly announced.

Greg congratulated her, then reached for the black powder. "The only one left is Eddy. Any ideas?"

Carrie was staring out the window to the yard next door. The whirr of an old-fashioned push lawnmower drifted up into the bedroom. "As a matter of fact, yes."

Eddy had been working for over an hour, if you could call it work. The moody 16-year-old took his time trimming around the flower beds. When Greg and Carrie wandered in through the gate, he was just getting up from a rest break in the hammock.

"Looks like you need a drink." Greg tried not to make it sound sarcastic. Carrie was behind him, carrying two plastic glasses on a tray, one filled with fizzy brown, the other with fizzy orange. "What do you want, cola or orange?"

"Cola." Eddy's eyes were full of suspicion. "What are you up to?"

"Just trying to be nice," Greg answered. "Sorry about not returning the video."

"No problem." Eddy smirked. Carrie was on his left side, forcing him to use his left hand to pick up the

glass. Greg drank from the other glass, paying
attention to the spot where Eddy's thumb was wrapped
around the plastic.

"So, how's it going?"

"Fine." Eddy finished it off in two swallows. Carrie's
tray was nearby when he lowered the glass and placing
it back there seemed only natural. As soon as the glass
was on the tray, the detectives made an about-face and
marched straight back to the Rydell yard.

Eddy stood by the hammock, frowning and scratching
his head as they disappeared. "Weird little brats."

*   *   *

Carrie had just lifted the third thumbprint with a clear
piece of tape. As she pressed the tape onto an index
card and labeled it, Greg took Eddy's plastic glass and
rinsed out the sticky scum of orange soda.

When all the index cards were ready, they sat down
at Greg's desk and compared, trying to match one of
the three thumbprints they collected to the print from
Aunt Mimi's box. "There's no match," Greg finally
whispered. "They're all different."

"They can't be," Carrie protested. "Let's check again."

They checked again and came up with the same

result. No match. "Someone else must have been in the house," Carrie said and threw the useless cards onto the bed. "Oh, Greg. We'll never solve this. Everyone's going to think it was me."

"That's impossible." Greg glanced around his bedroom. Somewhere they had made a mistake. But where? There on his bed were the index cards. Beside them were Eddy's plastic glass, the roll of tape, Becca's nail file and Aunt Mimi's box. Then he started to laugh.

"We're idiots." Greg started to dance around the room. "Total fools. I know where we made our mistake. I know who took the brooch. I know."

Carrie made a face. "How can you know?"

How did Greg know? The answer is right here in the story. When you think you know, too, turn to the solution on page 131.

For hints on how to lift fingerprints, turn to the "Fingerprints" section of **The Crime Solver's Handbook,** *at the beginning of this book.*

AUNT MIMI AND THE SWAMI

1. Secret Messages

Greg liked Aunt Mimi. She was rich and full of fun and always involved in some adventure. Like right now, he thought. How many other kids got to visit a real swami and take part in a seance?

It all began when Aunt Mimi telephoned his parents last week, asking if he could come up to New York. "The most perfect psychic lives just across the street," she chirped in her birdlike voice. "Gregory has to meet him. I insist." No one ever said no to Aunt Mimi. So, Greg packed a bag and waited for her chauffeur to pick him up in the big yellow taxi to take him from D.C. to New York.

Greg and his aunt sat at a table in the swami's colorful apartment while the tall, dark-skinned man with the turban and pointy beard polished his crystal ball with a cloth. "Mimi, dear," he said in a lilting Indian accent, "We will try once more to contact the spirit guide, Ama. Ama will guide you to your one true love."

"I was writing about love just this morning in my diary," Mimi exclaimed.

"Diary!" the swami repeated as he glanced out the nearby window. "Diary! Well, let's all hold hands and close our eyes." The swami shot his arms out of the sleeves of his robe, grabbed their hands, and began to hum. "Mmmm Ama! We lowly mortals are in need of your guidance." He was chanting in a singsong voice. It was kind of spooky and silly at the same time, Greg thought.

Even with his eyes shut, Greg couldn't help seeing the bright flash of light. More and more flashes hit his eyelids until finally he gently sneaked them open and looked out the window. Another flash, like sunlight bouncing off glass. It was coming from the high-rise apartment building across the street. Greg could see someone facing them, a blonde woman standing inside a fifth-floor window. Her right hand was raised and light seemed to be blinking from it. Quick flashes followed by short pauses, then more flashes. Dozens of them.

A delicate voice was coming out of the swami now, a woman's voice. "I am Ama, priestess of love. You seek guidance, dear soul. In your diary, you wrote of two men. Two old boyfriends. You wondered if one of these is your true life mate."

"Yes. That's exactly what I wrote," twittered Aunt Mimi.

"I am sorry. Neither man is your destined love. But

there is a third, a man named Henry."

"Henry? Henry Posley?" Aunt Mimi's lipstick curled into a frown. "My one true love? Hmm, I never quite trusted Henry. Maybe I was wrong."

When Greg sneaked his eyes open again, the flashes had stopped. The woman was still in the window, but now with binoculars, her gaze focused on Swami

Morishu. Behind the woman, Greg could see the snarling face of Rex, the favorite pet poodle Aunt Mimi had had stuffed and mounted and made into a table lamp. Wait a minute!

Greg blinked and looked again. It was Rex, all right, just as dead and dusty as ever. But if Rex was in the window, then the woman must be in Aunt Mimi's apartment. He inspected the other windows. Yes, it was Aunt Mimi's place. There was her gadget-filled kitchen and his own guest bedroom. The woman moved the binoculars in his direction and Greg snapped his eyes shut.

The seance lasted another half-hour, but he barely listened to any of it. What was that woman doing in his aunt's apartment? And why was she spying on them?

Greg didn't tell anyone about this. But two days later, after it happened again, he got on the phone to Carrie.

"On both days it was the same. The woman, the flashes of light, the binoculars. 1 didn't say anything. Our sessions are always at noon, when the maid and the chauffeur are out to lunch. So, no one else was in Aunt Mimi's apartment when the woman was there."

"Could be burglars," Carrie said.

"I thought so, too. I asked if anything's been missing lately and she said no. Look, Carrie, I gotta go. Aunt Mimi's cooking her famous octopus fondue. She needs me to stand by with the fire extinguisher."

The next seance was Sunday afternoon. Swami Morishu led them to the table by the window and once again instructed them to close their eyes.

"You wrote in your diary this morning." The swami was speaking to his aunt in Ama's high, singsong voice. "You wrote about love? No. You wrote about friends? No."

As before, the flashes of light hit Greg's eyes and, as before, he sneaked them open. There was the woman again, at Aunt Mimi's window. She held the binoculars to her eyes with one hand. From the other hand came the flashes.

"You wrote about family?" the swami continued. A single flash. "No. You wrote about money?" And, for the first time today, a double light flashed out. "Ah, yes. You wrote about money."

Suddenly it was clear. "She's signaling him," Greg thought. "She's using those binoculars to read his lips, then she's signaling him with a hand mirror. One flash for no. Two flashes for yes."

Aunt Mimi smiled. "I don't usually think about money, but yes. This morning I did."

So, that was it. They were working together. As soon as he and Aunt Mimi left the apartment, the woman sneaked in and started snooping. She read Aunt Mimi's diary, checked old phone messages, went through their bedrooms. That's how the swami knew. He wasn't psychic at all.

A bunch of new flashes. "Will," the high voice said eagerly. "You were thinking about your will."

"Not exactly," Mimi twittered. "I wasn't thinking about *my* will."

This fake and his partner were after her money. They had to be. But what could Greg do? Just as the next flash hit, Greg jumped to his feet. "I've got a headache," he pouted. And before the swami could stop him, Greg was at the window, pulling down the blinds.

"You can't do that," the psychic yelped suddenly in his real voice.

"Why?" Greg said accusingly. "Are you looking at something out there?"

"No. But I need the sun for my vibrations."

Aunt Mimi's eyes were open and she was rubbing her temples. "To be honest, swami. That flashing sunlight gives me a headache, too. Let's enjoy the shade for a minute. Ama didn't answer my question. Whose will was I thinking of?"

Greg grinned. "Yeah. Tell us about the will. And don't look out the window."

Beads of sweat began to appear under Swami Morishu's turban. "Uh, I can't contact Ama now." He was on his feet now, nervously pacing the floor. Every few seconds he would turn and stare at Greg, as if trying to figure out what the boy was up to. "Let's take a break."

The swami went into the kitchen and made iced tea. They drank it in the kitchen. Every now and then, the swami would bring up the will. But Greg would always change the subject before Aunt Mimi could say anything.

Time passed slowly. Half an hour later, after they'd all drunk their tea, Aunt Mimi was getting impatient. "Ama must be wondering what has happened to us."

Swami Morishu looked sick. And then the doorbell rang. The tall man almost ran to answer it. "Ah," he said from the doorway. "Food delivery. Uh, that's right. I ordered sandwiches from the corner deli. My treat."

Greg caught a glimpse of the delivery boy just before he walked away. Only it wasn't a he. It was a woman. A blonde. In fact, from what Greg saw, she looked just like the woman he'd seen at Aunt Mimi's window.

Swami Morishu was in a better mood now. He placed the big brown bag on the kitchen table and invited them to pick out their own sandwich.

Greg reached into the bag, still confused. Could it really be the same woman? And why was she delivering sandwiches? Absentmindedly, he pulled out a folded sheet of paper. Probably a deli menu or a receipt, he thought, and slipped it in his pocket. Reaching in again, he found a ham sandwich.

"Did anyone see ..." Swami Morishu was at the paper bag now, his head nearly buried inside. "Did anyone see a piece of paper? Greg? Maybe when you took out your sandwich?"

Greg almost admitted it but changed his mind. "You mean like a menu? No, I didn't see anything. Why?"

"Oh, no reason." The swami dove back into the bag, tearing out sandwiches and pickles and closely examining the pile of napkins. "Blast," he muttered under his breath. "Are you sure you didn't see a paper? Even a blank paper?"

"Nope." Greg took a big bite of ham, then secretly glanced down at the tip of paper sticking out of his pocket.

* * *

"He got real upset. And then he sent us home. He didn't even try to contact Ama. Aunt Mimi was sure mad." Right before dinner Greg was again on the phone to Carrie.

"They're con artists," Carrie decided. "Working together. Greg, you have to protect your aunt."

"They must have Aunt Mimi's apartment key. But how do they do the signals?"

"One flash for 'no.' Two flashes for 'yes.' When she needs to give him words, like *will*, she probably spells them out in Morse code. So, what about this piece of paper from the deli bag? What's on it?"

"Nothing." Greg held up the folded paper, as though he were showing it to her over the phone. "Blank. No writing on either side."

"No!" Carrie didn't believe it. "There must be something. I mean, as soon as you closed the blinds, she must have called the deli, ordered a bunch of sandwiches, then written a message to put inside the bag."

"Well, there's nothing on it," he insisted. "Unless it's invisible."

"Ooh. Good idea. Did you check for invisible writing?"

"What? I was kidding. How can writing be invisible?"

"Lemon juice," Carrie reported. "You take a tiny paintbrush, dip it in lemon juice, and write. When it dries, the writing turns invisible."

"Then how do you read it?"

"Simple." And she explained the technique.

Greg made Carrie stay on the line while he went into the living room. He switched on Rex, took off his lampshade, and held the paper up to the bulb the stuffed dog was holding between his paws. Brown letters quickly began to appear.

A minute later, Greg was back on the phone. "It's invisible writing, all right. But the message is nonsense. I mean it's in English letters but they aren't real words."

"Hmm. A secret code. The swami and his friend must have worked out a code, just in case something like this happened. Are there any letter patterns?"

"Patterns?"

"Small groups of letters that repeat. Look at the four-letter words."

Greg checked the message. "Yeah," he said, his voice regaining some hope. "The first word has repeating letters. XBXB."

"Good, that could be *Mimi*. It took Carrie a few seconds to grab a pencil and paper. When she was ready and back on the phone, Greg spelled out the message.

XBXB FSGCZ HEGWC OZS WLNPZ'K FBPP. OZ JBZJ PHKC DZHS. KOZ BLOZSBCZJ XGKC GQ OBK HKKZCK HLJ BK ZUZL SBNOZS COHL FZ COGWAOC. HXH.

"I'll work on it," she promised. "Meanwhile, take care of Aunt Mimi. This swami guy is up to no good."

Can you read the swami's message? For help, consult the "Codes" section of **The Crime Solver's Handbook.** *When you think you've correctly decoded the message, turn to the solution on page 132.*

The handbook also contains great information on "Invisible Ink," "Morse Code," and "Sending Messages with Mirrors."

2. Observing the Swami

Carrie stood in front of the swami's apartment building, talking to her new friend, "So, this swami doesn't have a lot of clients."

"Just two," the doorman replied. "There's that crazy rich woman across the street." He meant Aunt Mimi. "And then a nice-looking blonde." Carrie figured this had to be the swami's lady partner. "He never gets any other guests."

"Is that his real name? Swami Morishu?"

"Don't know." The doorman finally looked past Carrie and noticed Greg weaving through the traffic. "Hey!"

Greg had sneaked halfway across the avenue, then hidden himself behind a huge pot in the middle of the street divider. At a break in the cars, he raced across the rest of Park Avenue and started pawing through the bags of garbage on the doorman's curb.

"Hey, kid! What the heck is he doing?"

Before the doorman could move, Greg found what he was looking for. Among all the gray and black plastic, he grabbed the only green bag, then darted back across the avenue. A mail truck honked its horn and swerved. Carrie breathed a sigh of relief as Greg reached the far sidewalk.

"Crazy kid!" The doorman scratched his head. "Stealing garbage. That's a first."

A few minutes later, Carrie walked into Greg's bedroom. Greg had on a pair of long opera gloves that he'd rescued from his aunt's clothing drive donation and was rummaging through the open bag. "I can't believe I almost got run over for garbage. This stuff stinks."

Carrie put on a second pair of opera gloves and joined him. "Don't forget. We're looking for anything that tells us a little more about the swami. Aha!" Her first find was a cigar wrapper. "Panatela," she read, then placed it in a baggie and labeled it.

They had been on the first day of their stakeout, sitting by a window and using their own binoculars to watch the swami's apartment. Late that morning, when Carrie saw him tying up a green garbage bag, she got the bright idea to steal it.

"No personal mail," Greg said as he sifted through a stack of envelopes. "Occupant ... Occupant ... Hairbrush." He held up a black hairbrush.

Carrie eagerly grabbed it. "Hmm. The swami's hair is black. His partner's is blonde. Yours is brown. Aunt Mimi's is gray." Carrie used tweezers to pick a hair out of the brush then examined it with a magnifying glass.

"Red and wavy. What's a red, wavy hair doing in the swami's apartment?"

Greg wasn't paying attention. He had found two small triangles of foam rubber. The flat end of each triangle seemed to be dyed with a brown liquid. "What are these?"

Just bag and label it," Carrie said. "I'll look at it later." She herself was busy bagging and labeling the red hair.

"Hello in there. Yoo-hoo." It was Aunt Mimi. By the time she threw open the door, Greg and Carrie had stuffed the garbage out of sight behind the bed. "What's that smell? Gregory, did you brush your teeth?"

"Yes, Aunt Mimi."

"Good. Are you children ready for some adventure?" Mimi's eyes were aglow. "The swami and I just had a session. My spirit guide says today is critical. Ama gave me very detailed instructions. We walk three blocks north, chant to the sun for two minutes, take the first taxi heading west, then . . . .Well, the swami wrote it all down. At the end of our journey, at exactly three o'clock, I will encounter my true mission in life. Isn't that just too exciting?"

A few minutes later they were exiting Mimi's building, turning north. That's when Carrie happened to glance across the street and see the swami. He was dressed in a suit but still wore his turban. "This is our chance," she hissed. "I'm going to tail him."

"What?" Greg whispered back. "What am I going to tell Aunt Mimi?" But Carrie was already on her way, disappearing across the avenue, heading south after the turban.

* * *

"It's almost exactly three." Aunt Mimi went from checking her watch to checking Ama's list. They had taken three taxis, zigzagged across Times Square traffic while humming "Born Free" and even walked backwards for a block, just so they'd be facing the sun. She and Greg now stood exhausted, somewhere downtown on the Bowery, in front of a small Off-Off-Broadway theater.

"This is obviously our destination." Mimi looked into the box office window and was startled to see a surly young man with orange hair staring back. "Hello. Is there a show today?"

"If you can call it a show." The orange-haired boy pointed to a sign proclaiming *"The Marigold Prophecy. A new drama of spiritual importance."* "Matinee starts in two minutes," he said.

"Wonderful." Aunt Mimi beamed. "The spirits must want us to see it. Three tickets, dear." And then, for the first time since they left Park Avenue, Mimi glanced around. "Where in the world is Carrie?"

"Oh." In all the excitement, Greg had forgotten to tell his aunt about Carrie. Worse, he'd even forgotten to think up an excuse. "Uh, Carrie? She's around here someplace."

"Carrie!" Aunt Mimi shouted. "When did you last see her? You don't think when we were crisscrossing Times Square . . . ." Aunt Mimi shuddered. "Where's a phone? I'll call the police commissioner."

"No," Greg blurted. "I'm sure she's okay."

"Better yet, I know the President's unlisted number." And then her voice suddenly calmed. "Oh, there you are. Carrie, you gave us such a fright."

Greg jumped and turned. There was Carrie, all right, walking around the corner. Before she could reach them, he was racing to meet her. "Thank goodness. How did you know where to find us?"

"I didn't. I was following the swami. He walked into this place 10 minutes ago. I didn't have money to buy a ticket, and I didn't know what to do. The swami's instructions led you here? Very weird."

"Carrie, dear, you shouldn't wander off, not even for

a minute." Aunt Mimi was standing by the door, waving three tickets. "Well, come on. The play's about to start."

They walked into the theatre just as the lights were fading. Only about a dozen of the folding chairs were occupied. Carrie scoured the audience, looking for a tall head wrapped in a turban and seemed a little confused when she didn't see one.

"I know he came in here."

She was promptly hushed by Aunt Mimi, who was squinting at the program. "It can't be," Mimi gasped in a voice high enough to be a car alarm. A dozen heads turned in her direction. Two dozen eyes glared. And then the curtain went up.

It was the story of man who was searching the world for some rare flower. Along the way, he learned all sorts of lessons about life. The lead actor was a tall redheaded man who overacted a lot.

The whole thing seemed pretty silly. And then the scene changed to a flower shop. The woman behind the counter turned around and Greg instantly yelped, "That's her!" The flower woman was being played by the swami's blonde partner. "An actress."

Aunt Mimi sat entranced by the cheap sets and the bad acting. As the curtain fell on Act I, she turned to her nephew and gushed, "That was Henry Posley. You know, the old boyfriend Ama said was my one true destined love. It's fate. Fate! The spirits have led me to him."

Greg knew better than to argue, but something was definitely fishy. He didn't realize what it was until the second act when Carrie leaned across and whispered, "That red-haired actor. It's the swami."

"No." Greg tried to imagine that face with darker skin, black hair and a turban. "Well, maybe. Those foam pads I found. He could have used them for make-up."

"And the wavy red hair." Aunt Mimi hushed them again and they were forced to sit through the second act in silence.

"We have to go backstage," Mimi said. The house lights had come up and she began marching toward the stage. They ran to catch up, following her through the curtain and back to a row of dressing rooms. The name Henry was scrawled on a door.

Mimi knocked enthusiastically. "Yoo-hoo? Henry? This is a voice from your past."

"Mimi?" asked a voice. "Could that be Mimi Astorbilt? Uh, wait just a minute."

Carrie listened carefully. Someone was moving frantically inside. She could hear footsteps, things being knocked over. What was he doing? Finally, there was a shuffling sound, like something being crammed into a container.

"Darling!" The door flew open and there stood Henry, out of breath. "I saw you in the audience. What a wonderful surprise!"

Mimi led them into the small room and Henry introduced himself. "Ms. Astorbilt and I used to be such great friends—until she got the idea I was after her money. Don't deny it, Mimi.

It's normal for a rich woman to have such thoughts."
He kissed her on the cheek and she tittered. "After we
parted ways, I wrote a play. You were my inspiration. I
put every cent I had into this experimental tour de
force."

"You wrote it, too?" Mimi checked her program.
"Writer, producer, and star. How brilliant." Then she
gasped and gazed up to the ceiling. "This is what my
spirit guide wants. Oh, thank you, Ama." She turned
dramatically. "Henry, we are taking your show to
Broadway."

Henry seemed flabbergasted. "Are you serious? Me,
on Broadway? But that takes a lot of money."

"And I have a lot of money. The spirits said I would
discover my true mission, and this is it, to bring your
wondrous play to the world. The spirits have decreed.
Was I truly your inspiration?"

"My only inspiration." And he kissed her other cheek.

She tittered again. "What a day! Is there a financial
plan I can see?"

"It's right in the office." The eager actor was leading
her out the door. "Kids, make yourselves at home.
Your aunt and I have business to discuss."

The door slammed shut, leaving Greg and Carrie alone in the shabby dressing room. "That's him," Carrie said and pointed to a cigar in the ashtray. "Panatela, just like the swami."

Greg made a face. "Is she really going to do his show? It's terrible."

"It's all a con." Carrie began searching the cluttered room, turning over scripts and checking under costumes. "Henry and his girlfriend wanted to do their play. That's when he remembered Aunt Mimi. Henry knew she'd give him money, but he had to regain her trust."

Carrie disappeared into the closet and was rummaging around. "So, he disguised himself as Swami Morishu and spent a few weeks predicting her future."

"Hey. What are you looking for?"

"His disguise. When he came here today, he was the swami. His turban and wig and beard—they have to be somewhere."

"Good idea." Greg jumped up. "I'll start from this side. If we can show Aunt Mimi that Henry and Morishu are the same guy . . ."

Between them, they scoured the entire room, meeting in the center. They had found absolutely nothing. "He must have hidden it," Greg said and then snapped his fingers. "Sure. That's what he was doing when we knocked, hiding his costume. But where?"

Carrie eyed the door uneasily. "We'll use our powers of observation." She forced herself to stop searching and just look. Greg joined her in the center of the room. "He had to hide it in a hurry."

Inch by inch, they examined the dressing room, looking for anything out of place, any clue to the location of the costume. Any second now, Henry and Mimi might return.

Can you find the hiding place? Examine the illustration. When you think you've found the spot where Henry hid his disguise, turn to the solution on page 135.

Consult the **The Crime Solver's Handbook** *for information on "Hair and Fiber Analysis" and "How to Tail a Suspect."*

3. Canceling the Contract

"Yoo-hoo." It was the most depressed "yoo-hoo" they'd ever heard.

Aunt Mimi sighed her way into Greg's bedroom. "I am so bummed out." She plopped herself onto the bed. "Swami Morishu has left. His own guru called

him back to India. He's going to live in a cave and meditate, and I'm not going to have my swami anymore."

Greg was shocked. "You mean he's gone? Just like that?"

"Just like that. Moved out of his apartment this morning." A distant doorbell rang. "Who could that be?" Aunt Mimi slumped out of the room.

Greg turned to Carrie. "What do we do now? I mean, how do we prove Henry's the swami when there's no more swami? We can't let him just take her money."

Carrie frowned. "There's nothing illegal about getting someone to finance a Broadway show, even a lousy show."

They could suddenly hear voices from the living room, Aunt Mimi and a man. "We'll have an agreement written up, everything legal. After all, we don't want our affection for each other clouding our business judgment." It was Henry Posley, cooing romantically.

Greg and Carrie raced into the living room and found him stroking Aunt Mimi's hair. "Uh, we should hurry to the lawyer's office," Henry said as he worked to pull his fingers from the mass of hairspray. "No need for the children. They'll just be bored."

"We won't be bored," Greg protested.

"Henry's right. You stay home. Now where did I put my purse?"

"I'll get it." Greg ran out of the room, returning a minute later with Aunt Mimi's oversized handbag.

"Is my lucky pen in there?" She grabbed the bag and turned to Henry. "It was a gift from my very first guru. I can't sign any document without my lucky fountain pen."

"I doubt we'll be signing anything today." Henry swept an arm around her shoulder and guided her out the door.

Two hours later, Aunt Mimi returned home and dropped her purse into an empty fish tank. Greg was hiding behind the curtains. As soon as she disappeared, he fished it out and scurried back to his room. At the bottom of the overloaded purse, just where he'd planted it, was a cassette tape recorder. Greg rewound and pressed PLAY.

The first few minutes consisted of the ride downtown in Arthur's cab. Once they arrived at the lawyer's office, the sound got better. Henry introduced her to Jordan Harsh, a contract attorney, and Henry outlined the agreement they wanted. Aunt Mimi would put up all the money for *The Marigold Prophecy,* three million dollars. "We want the best production possible," Henry said.

When Mimi heard the price, she hesitated, "That's an awful lot. Perhaps my business manager should look at this."

Henry clucked his tongue. "He'll talk you out of it, I'm sure. Businessmen don't understand. I thought, when the spirits guided you to me, we could avoid all that negative nonsense."

"Yes, of course," Mimi apologized. "This isn't a business venture, it's a mission. All right, three million."

The lawyer worked out the details. Greg didn't know much about business, but it sounded like a pretty bad deal to him. "I can have it written up by tomorrow," Jordan Harsh announced. "Two P.M. And Ms. Astorbilt, please bring a checkbook. On signing, you'll need to pay Mr. Posley half a million dollars."

Carrie wandered in and Greg played the entire tape again. Then they sat on his bed trying to figure out what to do.

"Tomorrow," Greg moaned. "What can we possibly do by tomorrow?"

"We have to do something," Carrie said. "Is there some grown-up who can help us? Maybe one of her friends?"

Greg made a face. "Aunt Mimi has weird friends. Like this gourmet chef. Cal Encino. He lies all the time. He's her best friend, knows everything about her, but you never know when he's telling the truth."

* * *

Chef Cal Encino looked down at the spoonful of rice, then up at Greg. "You want me to chew on uncooked rice?"

"Please. It's a school project," Greg explained. "We're trying to see if people with sensitive tastes can tell the difference in uncooked rices. My Aunt Mimi says you have the best taste buds in New York."

The chef smiled. "In all North America. When I was 15, I won an international tasting competition. Youngest winner ever. And I had a cold."

They were in the kitchen of the chef's cafe. Carrie had laid out three spoons of uncooked rice, all looking the same. In fact, they all were the same, from the same rice box. But that wasn't the real point of the test. "Just put each spoonful in your mouth. Chew it a while. Then tell us which is the best."

Chef Encino smiled and followed directions. As soon as he started chewing the first portion of rice, Greg was

ready with a question. "So, do you know Henry
Posley? He used to be Aunt Mimi's boyfriend."

"Mmm," the chef mumbled between chews. "Real
nice fellow. An actor. Got married a few months
ago."

"What?" Carrie blurted. "He's married?"

"Someone important told me. I think it was the
mayor. I'm done with this sample." Carrie handed him
a bowl and watched carefully as he spit the rice into it.
"Dry," he said and reached for a glass of water.

"No," Carrie said. "No water."

"Ah. More of a challenge, huh? Very well."

As soon as the second spoonful was in the chef's
mouth, Greg continued. "Who did he marry? An
actress?"

"Yeah. Some actress he knew before Mimi. A blonde.
Mm, better texture. Nutty flavor." And he spat out
mouthful number two.

Carrie had read about this in a book. It was an
ancient Chinese lie detector. You make your suspect
chew on uncooked rice. If he's lying, then his
nervousness will cause his digestion to slow down. His
body will stop producing saliva and he won't be able to

spit out the rice. But Chef Cal Encino was spitting out rice just fine.

"Is he telling the truth?" Greg whispered as the chef picked up the third spoon. "I can't tell."

"It's not really a foolproof method," Carrie admitted. "But I'll bet Henry is married—and to his blonde partner."

"Number three is the best," Chef Encino said as he chewed. "Reminds me of the rice I used when I cooked a special banquet for the very last emperor of China." And he easily spat out the third sample.

* * *

All during lunch they worked on Aunt Mimi, trying everything from a toothache to tea leaves to get her to cancel the meeting. "Your horoscope says it's a bad day for signing things," Greg told her.

"Nonsense. I checked my horoscope. It's a great day. Now where's my lucky pen? Has anyone seen my pen?" Aunt Mimi's voice echoed as her head vanished into her huge purse.

"Here it is." Carrie walked into the room, wiping off the gold fountain pen with a towel. "You left it in the bathroom."

"Huh. Why was I using my lucky pen in the bathroom?" Mimi tossed it in her purse. "Is everyone ready? Today is the day Mimi Astorbilt becomes a Broadway producer."

Arthur and his yellow taxi-limousine were waiting, and within minutes Mimi and her young friends arrived at the lawyer's office. Henry was already there. "Oh. You brought the kids." And his manner became more defensive.

It was over quickly. The lawyer reviewed the contract. Every now and then Henry would eye Greg and Carrie suspiciously, but they simply sat on the couch, not saying a word. They continued to sit silently as Aunt Mimi brought out her lucky pen. She signed the last page with a flourish, then wrote out a check for half a million dollars.

Once they were out of the office and back in Mimi's private taxi, Greg spoke up. "Remember that errand I needed your help with?"

"Oh, yes," Mimi replied. "We'll do it right away. Arthur? Do you know where the Marriage License Bureau is?"

"Yes, ma'am. Centre Street. Don't tell me you and Mr. Posley are...?"

"Oh, no," Mimi giggled. "Not yet, anyway. You see, Carrie's cousin ran away from home. They think the young man moved to New York and got married. Our junior detectives are trying to track him down through his marriage records. Isn't that right, Carrie?"

"Uh-huh." It was amazing the things they could get Aunt Mimi to believe. "His name is Henny Iosley."

"Odd name," Mimi mused. "And somehow a little familiar."

The records were stored in the city clerk's office, a large room that was crowded with romantic couples applying for licenses. Aunt Mimi explained that they needed to look up a marriage certificate. The clerk nodded and had Carrie fill out a yellow form. "That'll be fifteen dollars," he told them.

Aunt Mimi turned over the money. "Just check the records for this year," she said, trying to be helpful. "Henny Iosley."

The clerk checked the name Carrie had written. He looked up, a bit puzzled. Then he shrugged and disappeared into a back room.

Ten minutes later he returned with a photostat copy

of a marriage certificate. "You were right," Mimi crowed. "One step closer to finding your cousin. Is there an address listed?" She grabbed the paper and started reading. "What a coincidence. Your cousin lives on the same street as Henry. Lives in the same building. Hmm." Her eyes roamed up the form and checked the name at the top. "Clerk." She was irritated. "Clerk! You looked up the wrong person. We don't want Henry Posley's marriage certificate. We want . . . . Oh. Oh, dear! Henry can't be married."

Greg watched her struggle with the proof that was staring her straight in the face. He should have felt happy about their plan working so well. Instead, he felt sorry.

"Henry's married," she finally said. Her voice wasn't weak or teary. It was strong and angry. "Why, that rat. Married! He was using me. Sweet-talking me into backing his idiotic play. Sorry, Carrie, we'll look up your cousin some other day. Where's a phone? I have to cancel that check."

Aunt Mimi almost flew, the sleeves of her dress flapping like wings. She found a pay phone in the lobby and was soon talking to the vice president of her bank. She gave him the check number, the name, and the amount. "Stop payment," she ordered and hung up. "Good." Then her victorious grin faded.

"What's wrong?" Greg asked.

"I signed something, didn't I?" Mimi sat herself down on the marble floor, opened her purse and pulled out her copy of the contract. "Oh, my," she murmured as she read. "According to this, I have to finance his play. There's no clause letting me change my mind. Oh, Gregory. Why did I ever sign?"

For the first time, Aunt Mimi looked defeated. Her wrinkled face, usually held up by a smile, was sagging into her neck. Greg couldn't resist a smile. "You tell her," he said to Carrie. "It was your idea."

A glimmer of hope flashed in Mimi's eyes. "What idea?"

"You don't have to pay anything," Carrie said proudly. "You never really signed the contract."

"Of course I did. There's my signature in dark blue ink."

"No, it isn't," Carrie laughed.

Aunt Mimi stared at her. "What have you children been up to? This is one of your little detective thingies, isn't it?" She was smiling again. "Tell me, tell me. I really don't have to pay off that smarmy con artist? How in the world did you manage it?"

How did Greg and Carrie foil Henry's con game? The method they used is described somewhere in **The Crime Solver's Handbook.** *When you think you've figured it out, turn to the solution on page 137.*

Consult **The Crime Solver's Handbook** *for "Lie Detecting Methods."*

SUMMER CAMP ALIENS

1. The Disappearance

The full moon ducked behind a cloud. Good. Greg and Carrie took deep breaths then popped up from behind the rock and ran.

Carrie kept one hand up, protecting her face from the oncoming branches. Out of the corner of her eye, she saw something move. In that bush. She turned her head, all the time still running. "Greg?" But Greg was ten feet ahead and pulling away. "Someone's there." And she stopped.

Greg looked back. The moon was just emerging. "Run. You're a target." But it was too late. He saw her gasp as the force of the shot snapped back her head. Suddenly Carrie's face was a blob of red. Red liquid covered her eyes and dripped down her cheeks.

Greg pressed himself flat against a tree. He didn't dare look, didn't dare move, not until he heard the killer's gleeful peel of laughter and the footsteps running away. Then he scrambled back to Carrie's side. "Are you all right? I mean for being dead?"

Carrie was taking off her goggles, wiping her face, and doing her best to keep the paint from getting on her jacket. "I hate this game."

This was Greg's first year at summer camp and Carrie's second. One of the big events was a nighttime game of Capture the Flag. Camp Potomac divided itself into red and blue teams. Each camper was given goggles and an armband, while each team was supplied with ten paint guns. The paint guns usually went to boys, older boys with a few summers' worth of experience.

"Looks like someone got killed," a voice called out. Greg spun around, ready to dive for a rock. But it was only Ping Lao, Greg's tentmate, sporting a blue armband, just like theirs, and a blue paint gun. Ping was a year older than Carrie, a nice guy who loved pranks and practical jokes even more than Greg. "What're you doing way out here?"

Greg pointed to the fence. "We were hoping to scoot outside camp property and in again at the archery range. It's right by the red flag."

"Highly illegal." Ping was planning to be a lawyer like his father, head legal counsel at the Chinese embassy. "I like it." He bent down and refastened the adhesive bandage that covered a cut on his leg. "That's the McGruder farm," he added, gazing beyond the fence. "You guys aren't scared to go there? You know, all the ghost stories they tell around the campfire."

"Please!" Carrie laughed. "That's just their way of keeping campers off his land."

"Oh, yeah? What about that guy a few months ago? Some old hermit just disappeared. Without a trace."

"Wow!" Greg was getting the chills. "You think the ghosts got him?"

"There are no ghosts," Carrie sneered. "Anyway, the rules say I have to go back. Have fun." And she walked away.

A mischievous twinkle appeared in Ping's eye. "Well, Greg. If you're not scared of a few ghosts, neither am I. You ready?"

"What? You wanna go with me?" Greg was suddenly partners with an old pro, and a shooter, too. "All right!" He let Ping take the lead, following him over the wooden fence and into a new set of woods.

Five minutes later, they came out on a hill overlooking a lake they'd never seen before. They were somewhere on McGruder's farm. Lost. They strained to see some trace of the camp, but nothing looked familiar. A dog snarled and barked in the distance and Greg remembered the campfire stories about Old Man McGruder's wolfhound. His skin began to crawl.

It was Ping who first saw the humanlike creatures. All four were floating, maybe even walking, across the mist-covered lake. Large white heads with bug eyes and huge round mouths. Their bodies too were white, almost glowing. Ping gulped. "Wow! Aliens."

"Aliens?" Greg was stunned—and a little relieved they weren't ghosts. On the shore, a red light strobed from a shadowy machine. "Look. More. Coming out of the ground."

Not far from the machine, two white heads had popped up, followed by bodies that slowly climbed out onto the scrubby soil. Not human. They could see that much, despite the spinning red light and the mist. "Wow," Greg said and this time his voice carried.

One of the aliens looked their way. There was no place to hide. The creature pointed right at them and a white light flashed from his finger. Ping and Greg both felt frozen, caught in the beam. Then, somehow, they managed to turn—and run.

* * *

Carrie was dubious. "There's got to be a logical explanation."

"Yeah? What?" Greg challenged. "You didn't see them. We did."

They hadn't told the counselors. Their fear of breaking the rules was, for now, stronger than their fear of aliens. All three of them sat huddled in Greg and Ping's tent, the boys telling and retelling what they saw and trying to figure out what to do.

"All right, boys. Lights out," a grown-up voice bellowed out of the darkness. It was Todd Grisham, Toady Todd, the water sports counselor. He came closer. "Who is that? Lao? Rydell? You guys have a girl in there?"

After taps, girls and boys had to stay separate. Those were the rules. Todd did his expected bout of yelling, then marched Carrie across to the girls' side of the camp. Greg and Ping watched them disappear, then switched off their flashlights. "We'll talk in the morning," Greg yawned, "when our heads are clear. What a night, huh?"

* * *

Anna Fox, the crafts counselor, sat in the doorway of her tent. She hailed Greg as he passed. The heavy-set woman had just finished making a pair of moccasins and her mouth was still full of rawhide laces that needed to be cut. "Where's your tentmate?" she chewed.

"Don't know. He wasn't around when I got up."

"Hmm. Ping said he would help me with the lanterns

for tomorrow's campfire. It's not like him to stand me
up." She pulled her head back and the laces went taut.
"Give me your pocket knife." Greg didn't have one. So,
with her free hand, Ms. Fox pulled a lighter from her

pocket, flicked the flint, and singed through the laces. "Just like a Native American," she said proudly. "They didn't have pocket knives either."

At the mess hall, Toady Todd was taking roll. That's when they discovered Ping was missing. Ten senior campers fanned out across the Potomac property and each returned with the same story. No one had seen him all morning.

The sheriff's office took the news seriously. "There was a

local man who vanished three months ago," the sheriff explained. "Never found. I know this missing kid is a bit of a prankster. But we're treating this as a real disappearance, maybe even a kidnapping."

Greg had his own ideas. What if the aliens had come and disintegrated Ping? Or taken him back to their planet? Greg ran off to confer with Carrie. He found her at the pond, dangling her legs in the water.

"Don't be an idiot," Carrie said as nicely as possible. "There are no aliens. I'll bet anything he just sneaked onto McGruder's farm and got lost. We should go back up to the lake and look for him."

"Yeah. Good plan," Greg said, even though going back to the lake was the last thing he wanted to do. He was about to say something else when there was a rustle of branches coming from a row of lilac bushes. A faint scent of cigarette smoke mixed with the lilacs and, for a moment, they felt uneasy, as if they were being spied on.

They didn't have a chance to put their plan into action until after lunch.

Carrie brought her copy of *The Crime Solver's Handbook* and met Greg by his tent. She was surprised to find him 10 yards from the edge of the meadow, on his hands and knees, pawing through the dirt. "What are you doing?"

Greg looked up, excited. "Remember the cut on Ping's leg?" He pointed to a small drop of dried reddish black on the dusty ground. "What do you think?"

"Blood," she said under her breath and began to look around for more. "A blood trail." Greg joined her and in less than a minute they'd found another circular drop, this one on the leaf of a sumac sprig. "He went this way."

Carefully, they lined up the two drops and went in a straight line, following one of the many paths through the woods. Every 20 yards or so, they would find another drop. Some were easily visible on rocks. Others were on leaves or on the ground. Occasionally, there would be no drop for 40 to 60 yards, then they would find several bunched together.

"We're going the wrong way." Carrie came to a halt and scratched her head. "We're heading away from the McGruder farm. Why would Ping come this way? It doesn't make sense." She pulled the handbook from her pocket and began to flip through.

"I found another one," Greg called out and waited for her to catch up.

They examined the new blood drop, spread over a few pebbles. Like the others, it was symmetrical and relatively round. "They're fakes," Carrie announced.

"What do you mean, fakes? You mean Ping planted these blood drops?"

"Not Ping. Someone else. Someone who wants us to go in this direction. Blood doesn't make this shape, not unless it's falling straight down and the person's standing still. Here. Read this chapter."

Greg read it through twice and nodded. "You're right."

"Someone is leading us off on a wild goose chase."

Greg frowned. "I don't get it. I mean, what's the point? Why would someone want to send us on a false trail?"

"Yeah," Carrie agreed. "What's the point?"

They lowered themselves onto a tree stump and thought. If someone was making a false blood trail, that meant Ping didn't just get lost. Someone had done something to him and was now trying to lead people away from the real location.

"You think someone kidnapped him?" Greg asked. "You think maybe the aliens?"

"There are no aliens," Carrie growled. "Someone heard us. Someone—a human—was in the bushes and heard us planning to go to McGruder's. The person didn't want us going there, so he set up this phony trail."

"Let's go tell the sheriff," Greg said and led the way back along the trail. When they emerged onto the quadrangle of platform tents that made up the boys' field, a dozen officers were spread out on the nearby grass, bent over and inspecting the ground. "Uh-oh," Greg said. "They found it, too."

A moment later, the camp director saw Greg and Carrie. "This area is closed to campers right now," Lucas Miller told them. "The sheriff's men found something."

"It's fake," Carrie interrupted. "You found blood drops, right? Well, they're fake. It's a wild goose chase to make you go the wrong way."

Mr. Miller was one of the good guys, friendly and usually willing to give you the benefit of the doubt.

Now he didn't look so friendly. "Did you make these blood drops? Is that what you're saying?"

"No," said Carrie. "But we examined them. They're too round and even. Someone wants to lead you in the wrong direction."

"Carrie." Lucas Miller was rubbing the light brown stain on the inside of his middle finger. "You're a smart girl. But why don't we leave the police work to the police?" And without another word, he shooed them off the field.

"I hate it when people don't listen," Carrie muttered. "Come on." She was already leading Greg across the camp, to the pond and the lilacs. Pushing aside the leafy branches, she began to inspect the ground. "Aha! A fresh footprint, in the middle of a lilac bush! I told you someone was spying on us." A cigarette butt also caught her eye. "Whoever spied on us is a smoker. Probably a counselor, since they're pretty careful about keeping cigarettes away from campers."

Greg picked up the butt. "Good work. Now what counselors do we know who smoke?"

Which counselors smoke? Test your powers of observation by trying to solve this one without reviewing the story. And remember, you don't have to actually see someone smoke to know he's a smoker. When you think you know, check the solution on page 138.

Consult **The Crime Solver's Handbook** *for more information on "Blood Evidence."*

2. The Rescue

Ping was slowly coming to. He tried to open his eyes but couldn't. He tried to speak but couldn't. What had the aliens done to him? His head ached and his mind was so groggy. Last night...what happened last night?

He had waited until Greg was asleep. How could anyone sleep with aliens just over the hill? Ping certainly couldn't. It didn't take him long to find the lake. It looked so peaceful. No mist. No strobe lights. No aliens.

"Who are you?" It was a deep, Darth Vader voice, processed through some kind of breathing apparatus. Ping spun around, caught a glimpse of the white figure—bug eyes, hockey-puck mouth—and he was off, dashing past the alien, stumbling down the hill. And then he fell. That was the last thing he remembered: the fall. And now he couldn't open his eyes or mouth or...

Ping calmed himself. No, he wasn't mute and blind. He was gagged, bound and blindfolded. He was indoors, probably in a barn, judging from the smell. Then he heard the voices.

"The men finished last night," someone whispered. "It's all buried, safe and sound." The other voice was too soft to make out. "'Course it's safe. You think I'd let them plant all that toxic waste on my property if it wasn't?" Was that Old Man McGruder? "You saw all the cement. These guys are pros. Besides, they paid me enough. I'll retire and sell the farm. You think your campers would like a new field full of toxic waste?"

"Your campers?" Ping wondered. "Who is he talking to? Someone from the camp?" He suddenly smelled a cigarette.

"Don't smoke in my barn. How much do you think the kid saw?" Another

pause. "Well, we can't take any chances. It won't be the first time we got rid of a nosy neighbor. Hey, don't get squeamish. You had your chance to be a hero. Instead you took their money." McGruder laughed and Ping's skin crawled. "The police are following that fake blood trail. By the time they check out the farm, that Chinese kid'll be buried with the waste."

Ping sat frozen. Then the voices were gone. Nothing but the contented shuffling of cows. Ping moved his head around until it nudged up against something hard and metallic. It was a rake. He maneuvered it under the edge of his blindfold and pulled. After several tries, Ping moved the blindfold enough to catch a peek.

The first thing he saw was a skinned alien. No. His heart settled. Just a white, plastic suit hanging from a peg. It was the kind of protective suit that covered your whole body, with bug-eyed plastic goggles and a round filter over the mouth. They weren't aliens, just environmental polluters.

Ping thought it through: Take away the mist and the spooky night, and all you had were a bunch of men in boats and earth-moving machines, burying toxic waste and checking things out with a high-powered flashlight. He felt stupid and a little disappointed.

* * *

Greg and Carrie never found the lake. Instead, they found a house and barn. Coming to the edge of a field, hidden from view by cornstalks, they watched as someone drove away in a Camp Potomac pickup. A craggy-looking man was sitting on the porch, a rifle resting on his knees. Sleeping beside him was a wolfhound. McGruder's dog. Greg was more afraid of him than of the man himself.

Rain clouds were coming fast and the last rays of sun were just lighting up the barn. Then they saw it: a flash. It was a dull flash, barely noticeable. Then again. On the third flash, they pinpointed the source, a barn window. Greg undid his knapsack and pulled out binoculars. "There's someone inside, at the window."

"Yeah, a cow."

"No, a person." A fourth flash, then the sun was

swallowed up in clouds. "It came from his mouth."
Greg adjusted the binoculars' focus and felt a raindrop.
"It looks like there's some shiny tape on his mouth."
Greg's voice cracked. "It's Ping." The wolfhound on the
nearby porch pricked up his ears and began to growl.
"Let's get back."

They retreated into the corn, then sat down and
planned Ping's rescue. "We need a diversion,
something to keep the man and the dog busy." Greg
peered through the stalks and saw a herd of cows
wandering up to a pond. "Hmm." He reached into his
knapsack and pulled out a paint gun.

His diversion took another five minutes to organize.
A heavy rain began falling as Greg crawled back to the
edge of the field. Carrie was right behind him. "This
isn't going to hurt them," he promised. "You ready?"

The gun popped softly. A blue blob exploded on the
rear end of a Guernsey, and the cow reacted with a
terrified moo. The cows around her also reacted. A
second pop, and a second blue blob splattered over
two more cows. More terrified moans and moos. By
the fourth paint ball, the herd was in full panic,
colliding with each other as they stumbled away from
the cornfield.

The old man was suddenly on his feet, looking almost as panicked as the cows. "What's the matter? Calm down." Meanwhile, the dog was off the porch and barking furiously.

The frightened herd settled on a direction, toward the house, and they were gaining speed. "Hey!" The man waved his arms, then scrambled for his rifle and fired a shot in the air. The dog howled. A chorus of moos, the loudest yet. The stampede veered to the right, away from the house, thundering through a vegetable garden. The snarling dog followed, saliva flying from his mouth.

The man cursed, running after them into the rain. That's when Carrie took off across the grass and into the barn. It took her only seconds to find the window and climb in to rescue Ping. She tore the tape from his mouth and started working on the ropes. "They were going to kill me," the older boy sputtered. "What's going on out there?"

Carrie didn't explain but led him to the barn door and listened, her eyes focused down. A nearly unsmoked cigarette lay stubbed out on the floor. A used match lay a few inches away. "One of the counselors was here," Ping whispered. "I couldn't see which one."

Carrie nodded. "That was way cool, the way you used the tape as a signal."

"What signal? I was trying to look out the window."

"Well, it was still cool." Carrie poked her head through the barn door. "Let's go." And they raced away.

By the time the campers had finally sneaked their way back to the other side of the fence, the downpour had stopped. Along the route, Ping filled them in about McGruder and the toxic waste. Greg was amazed by Ping's story and couldn't wait to tell the police. Rescuing the son of a Chinese diplomat and exposing a band of toxic dumpers—they were heroes.

But things don't always work out. Greg knew something was wrong when he saw the man, Mr. McGruder, getting out of a pickup truck. His hands were covered in blue paint as he started talking to the sheriff and Lucas Miller. The men all saw the campers and didn't look happy.

"There they are," McGruder shouted. "I found one of them, that Chinese boy, hiding in my barn. He'd been

there all night. I grabbed him for trespassing. He kept talking about some practical joke. I was just going to call the camp when this other crazy boy, he starts shooting at my cows with a paint gun." He pointed to Greg, who was still carrying the weapon.

Mr. Miller frowned. " Did you shoot paint at his cows?"

"Yes," Greg stammered. "But it was self-defense."

"They kidnapped Ping," added Carrie. "They were going to kill him."

"Kill him?" Mr. Miller looked shocked. "Why in the world...?"

"Because of the toxic waste," Greg blurted. "McGruder and one of the counselors are in it together. We thought they were aliens. That's why we didn't tell anyone. But they weren't aliens, just men wearing special suits to bury the poison." Greg had a feeling of how stupid this sounded, but he kept going. "When Ping sneaked back to the farm, they kidnapped him. I had to shoot the cows as a diversion. "

"Lucas?" The sheriff cleared his throat then gazed at Ping. "Is this the same boy who set off the fireworks in the girls' latrine last year?"

"Yep," said Mr. Miller sadly. "Your parents aren't going to be very happy."

Greg, Carrie, and Ping all protested their innocence. "Go look on his farm," Carrie demanded. "Down by the lake. It's buried there, tons of toxic waste. All the proof you'll need."

"Shut up and go into the mess hall," the sheriff

ordered. "We'll deal with you in a minute."

It was a half-hour later when Toady Todd Grisham walked in to get them. "I hear you guys are in big trouble," he said gleefully. "Serves you right for missing my canoe races."

"Canoe races?" Greg had forgotten about the races, Todd's favorite event of the week.

"Yeah. And don't say you skipped it because of the rain. It didn't start raining until we were nearly through. They want you losers out by the flagpole. Now."

The sheriff and a deputy were waiting and quickly escorted the campers to the roped-off area around Greg and Ping's tent. As the sheriff untied the rope, Greg looked down and noticed the footprint. "Someone's been in our tent," he whispered.

Carrie saw it, too, an adult-size print outlined in the mud just outside the left flap. She hurried ahead, then stopped, preventing anyone from stepping on it. "Wait out here," the sheriff ordered, then walked around her into the tent.

The sheriff started his search from one side, the deputy from the other. When the deputy got to Greg's toilet kit, he inspected it carefully, then motioned to his boss.

"Okay, boys. Game's over." The sheriff reached into the kit, pulling out a small bottle of red liquid and an eyedropper. "Is this is how you made the blood drops?"

Greg was stunned. "That's not mine, honest. I've been framed. "

"Framed? You been watching too much TV."

"No." Greg pointed to the footprint. "You see that? That's proof. Someone was here after the rain stopped. They crossed the police ropes and planted that in my kit."

The sheriff wasn't listening. "We'll have this analyzed to see if it matches what's on the trail. Offhand, I'd say you three are facing expulsion, maybe even criminal charges." He and his deputy walked off, leaving Greg, Carrie, and Ping to worry about the future.

"This isn't fair," Ping complained. "They bury tons of poison, kidnap me, try to kill me, and we get arrested. Greg, what are you doing?"

The younger boy was bending over the footprint. "There must be some way to use this print as evidence.

Where's the handbook?" Carrie pulled the thin book out of her pocket. Greg took it, sprawled out on his cot and found the right page. "We'll make a cast of the footprint and compare it to everyone's shoes."

"We probably should make a cast," Carrie agreed. "But we already know who the crooked counselor is."

Greg was amazed. "And how do we know that?"

"Process of elimination," she replied. "We know a few more things about our suspects now. I think we can safely eliminate two of them."

Can you eliminate two of them? Review the story and see if you can narrow it down to one suspect. When you think you know, check the solution on page 140.

Consult **The Crime Solver's Handbook** *for information on "Footprint Evidence."*

3. The Evidence

Greg brushed the last clumps of dirt from the plaster cast. "It's a Supersonic Flyer," he confirmed, pointing out the double "S" in the tread. "A new pair, too."

Without exchanging a word, all three campers thought of the new pair of Supersonic Flyers that had arrived for Lucas Miller in Monday's mail.

"It's not him," Ping shouted. It can't be. I don't care what your footprints say. You don't know Mr. Miller. I've come here three summers and . . ."

Something splattered against the canvas, shaking the whole tent and making them jump. "Hey, Ping Pong," someone yelled. They knew that bullying voice— Butch Cleaver, a fourth-year camper and captain of the red team. "Played one too many jokes, huh? Your folks are coming for you." No one answered and no one looked outside to see what he'd thrown.

They thought it through and came up with a plan. The best way to prove their story was to expose the toxic waste. "We'll go back to the lake and do some digging," Ping suggested. "All we have to do is hit the top of the cement.

People are bound to wonder why McGruder buried a patch of cement by his lake."

It was late afternoon when they packed up the knapsack and slipped out under the tent's rear canvas. "How about a paint gun?" Greg whispered.

"Paint gun?" Carrie scolded. "That's how we got into this mess." But both boys insisted, and they started their mission by making a detour to steal a red paint gun from the supply tent.

Ping led them directly to the lake and they quickly found the large area of freshly turned dirt. Even though the toxic waste was buried under a mound of concrete, Carrie made them put on breathing masks and plastic gloves before they started. They took turns with the shovel, pitching out mounds of earth until they had a waist-deep hole.

It was Ping's turn to dig and he stopped when he heard the noise. "What's that?" They all listened. It was louder now. A dog barking. Angry barks that grew louder and closer. "Oh, no! McGruder's dog."

Suddenly there it was, barreling from around the edge of the woods. It saw them as soon as they saw it and dug in its heels, stopping just 20 feet away. The shaggy wolfhound faced them, saliva dripping from its teeth and its back hairs bristling.

For a minute nothing happened but the snarling and barking. Carrie saw Greg out of the corner of her eye. He was looking at the paint gun. "Greg, don't. He knows guns. He'll attack before you can even aim." Then she turned to Ping. "What are you doing?"

The older boy had taken off his mask and was inching toward the knapsack. "I'm going for a cupcake."

"How can you eat at a time like this?"

Ping reached into the sack as he continued to stare down the dog. "Nice boy," he said gently. "Chinese dogs are always hungry. You hungry?" Slowly, he pulled out a cupcake, unwrapped it, and held it out. "Doggie treat." He lobbed it with an underhand swing and it fell a few inches in front of the muddy, matted forepaws.

The dog sniffed at it, then snapped his head up, as if he were expecting some kind of trick. "Poor thing. Probably been mistreated. It's okay, boy."

The wolfhound sniffed again, then in one quick motion snapped up the cupcake. "Good boy," Ping said. "Want another?" The dog cocked its head and seemed to smile.

A second cupcake followed the first, followed by three strips of beef jerky. All the while, the dog never moved except for the few inches it took to reach the treats. "No more," Ping finally said. "Sorry. Please don't eat me."

The wolfhound cocked its head again and whined. Then, as quickly as it appeared, the dog whirled and bounded off. As it vanished behind an abandoned shack, the kids came to life.

Carrie sat down on a rock, her knees still wobbly. "I guess we keep digging. You'd think we would've found something by now." And it was just then she did find something. It was lodged deep in a berry bush, a faded red baseball cap, cracked and torn by the weather.

Greg bent over the bush. "Probably one of the toxic dumpers," he said. But Ping reminded him that they'd been wearing a different kind of headgear. "Well, then, probably McGruder. Looks like it's been here for months."

Carrie was still wearing gloves as she picked up the cap and placed it in a large plastic bag. "It could be evidence. You guys keep digging. I'm going to make a crime scene sketch."

"What?" Greg complained. "What good will that do?" "For later. To remind us how things are situated—where we found the cap, et cetera. The police do it all the time."

Carrie retrieved her pencil and sketchpad from the knapsack, sat back down on her rock, and drew. It took some time, since she wanted to make everything as accurate as possible. She was just returning her pad to the knapsack when the dog bounded down towards them again. "Oh, no. He's coming for more food."

Ping squinted. "No. He's already got something."

Once more the dog came to a halt, this time under an oak tree. The thing in its shaggy mouth was long and white, with knobs on both ends. "Like a baton," Carrie thought, and then her stomach turned. "It's a bone."

"He wants to play." Ping moved a foot closer, but the dog curled its lip and snarled.

"I wouldn't get too close." Greg grabbed Ping by the belt and pulled him back. The wolfhound lowered its lip and dropped the bone. Then it barked once, whirled around, and galloped away.

The bone had fallen onto a patch of grass and leaves. "Looks like a leg," Carrie deduced. "Too long and straight for an animal bone."

The boys knew what she was implying. They both made faces. "That's gross," Greg said. "I suppose you'll want to bag this, too?"

"Uh-huh." Carrie pulled out the largest bag, using it to pick up the bone. Some debris was sticking to it. "Dry gravel, dry soil, dog hair, oak leaf, raspberry thistle." She tried to get all of it into the bag, but the gravel and soil were so dry that much of it wouldn't stick. These bits she also saved, slipping them into a sandwich bag.

The sun was now low in the sky. They were tired and hungry. "I don't think we can dig down far enough to find the cement," Ping said, defeated.

Carrie and Greg agreed and started to pack up. "What if it *is* a human bone?" Carrie asked. "You know, that local guy who disappeared a few months ago?" She was trying to cheer them up, but it wasn't working.

They removed their masks and gloves, then headed

back to camp the same way they came. Soon they could see the fence and, with a rush of relief, they moved toward it.

"Stop right there!" It was a voice from their nightmares. McGruder's voice. "You kids never learn, do you?" He was right in front of them, stepping out from behind a tree. A rifle was slung over his forearm. "What're you doing on my property?"

"Nothing." Ping's voice quivered and his grip on the knapsack tightened.

McGruder saw this and smiled. "Nothing, huh? Put down the gun." It took Greg a second to realize he still had the paint gun. He lowered it to the ground. "What you got in the backpack?"

Before they could even reply, he shot out an arm and grabbed the knapsack. Then he sat on a stump and opened it, all the time using his free arm to keep the rifle aimed. "Now what have we here?" Feeling around inside, he pulled out a plastic bag and held it up to the fading light. An old cap. Looks like..."

His smile vanished. He eyed the campers warily, then reached in again. Another plastic bag, this one almost as long as the knapsack. "A bone," he said. For the longest time he sat quietly, his gaze going back and forth between the plastic bags and his prisoners. When he finally spoke, his voice was hoarse. "Where did you get these?"

"Down by the lake. Where you left them," Carrie answered, half-guessing.

McGruder looked as if he'd just been punched. "How'd you know about Sammy?"

Sammy. Carrie figured that had to be the local man who disappeared. She turned to Greg. "I told you it was a human bone. Sammy must've seen the toxic dumpers, too."

McGruder jerked to his feet and cocked the rifle. "Pretty darn smart. All right, girlie, put the stuff in the bag. Careful and slow." Carrie did as she was told.

"McGruder! What the heck are you doing?" The three youngsters turned their heads and saw Lucas Miller climbing over the fence. The camp director seemed to take instant control of the situation. "Put down that rifle."

Ping grinned and nudged Carrie. "I told you," he said. "Mr. Miller, am I glad to see you."

"Shut up," Lucas Miller barked.

McGruder was still aiming the rifle. "I guess our burial spot wasn't so good, Miller. They stumbled over Sammy's remains."

"Blast," Lucas said. "I never bargained for this kind of mess."

Even though they had deduced that Mr. Miller had to be the crooked counselor, the kids were still shocked. It was during this shocked silence that Greg

saw his opportunity and took it. He lunged forward, grabbing the knapsack with one hand and preparing the other to catapult himself over the fence.

In a second, he was inside the camp and racing down a wooded path. Every hundred feet or so, the paths would split and one after another he took new paths, almost without thinking. Any minute now, he

would run into a counselor and be safe. They wouldn't kill Carrie or Ping, not until they caught him.

A few more quick turns and he hit a clearing. Then came the ravine and the rope bridge. Greg glanced down at the rocky creek below, then up at the opposite bank. Farmer McGruder was standing there, out of breath but smiling, with his rifle at his side. "Throw me the backpack, boy."

Greg looked behind him for escape. But the wolfhound was suddenly there, snarling, its forepaws on the edge of the ravine.

"Looks like you're caught between a man and his dog," McGruder laughed. "Rufus, shut up!" Rufus snarled more than ever. "Okay, boy, throw me the sack and I won't have to shoot."

"You won't shoot," Greg yelled.

"Oh, I'm not aiming at you. I'm aiming at Rufus. Everyone knows how mean that dog is. You see, Rufus just attacked you. I'm trying to save your life. Unfortunately, I'm gonna miss him and hit you. Now time is running out. Throw me the sack."

"No." Greg could hear people shouting somewhere in the distance.

"All right, boy. I hate to do this. Gunshots drive that dog crazy." In a skillful sweep, McGruder raised the gun and aimed. Rufus saw the gun being pointed in his direction and, sure enough, went crazy.

Greg barely saw what was happening, it was all so fast. One second the dog was there, frothing at the mouth; the next second he was scrambling down the ravine and up the other side.

"No, you fool mutt." McGruder threw down his rifle and raised his arms to his neck. But the dog was already on him, everywhere on him, a swirl of snarling and biting.

McGruder's screams were muffled by his arms, making it easier for Greg to hear the shots. "Pop! Pop!" Rufus's backside was suddenly covered in red. "Pop! Pop!" Two more red bursts appeared, one on McGruder's chest, the other on the dog's head.

Rufus ran off in a whimpering, whiny confusion while McGruder slumped to the ground, still screaming for his life. "You shot me. I'm dying."

Greg spun around and recognized the shooter standing on the far bank. "Carrie!"

"I still hate this game," Carrie said as she lowered the paint gun. "But I *am* pretty good at it."

* * *

Greg's and Carrie's parents drove in that evening, expecting to find their children expelled. Instead, they found the camp director in handcuffs and the sheriff in a serious conference with the members of the Detective Club.

The sheriff was acting friendlier than Carrie had ever seen him. "I sent your bags off to Washington. A forensic geologist will study the stuff on the bone. That'll help us figure out where to dig for the body." He cleared his throat. "Mind me asking what that is?"

Carrie had unfolded her crime scene sketch. "It's a map I drew. The area where we found the cap." She looked up. "I examined the bone before I bagged it.

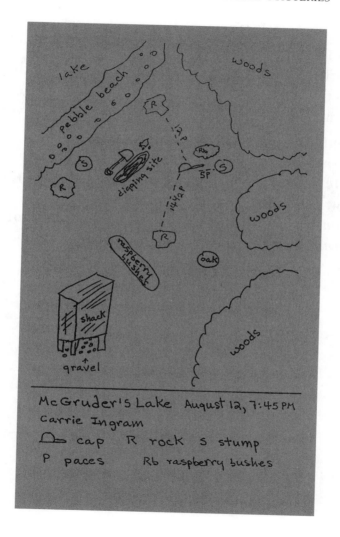

And I think I know where the body is."

"How can you possibly?" The sheriff controlled himself. "Well, far be it from me to second-guess the Detective Club. Would you kindly share your insights with me?"

Examine Carrie's sketch and compare it to the evidence she saw on the bone. Can you discover where Sammy's body is buried? When you think you know, check the solution on page 141.

Consult **The Crime Solver's Handbook** *for more information on "Crime-Scene Sketches."*

SOLUTIONS

Fingerprinting Fools Solution (page 32)

Greg picked up Eddy's index card. "This is *my* left thumbprint, not Eddy's."

"What?" Carrie's face brightened. "Are you sure?"

"Positive. We must have mixed up the glasses. Eddy drank the cola. I had the orange soda. Remember?" Greg turned to look at the tray and the empty cola glass on top of it. "Eddy's print is on that glass. And I'll bet you anything..."

Five minutes later, they had dusted and protected and examined the new print. It perfectly matched the tape from Aunt Mimi's box.

With this evidence in hand, they finally went to Greg's mom and told her everything.

Dr. Rydell examined the prints and listened to their story. "I'll go have a talk with Eddy's mother. I wouldn't have suspected you anyway, Carrie." She put the index cards in an envelope. "How did you do it? You kids have some sort of detective club? Is that it?"

"Detective club," Greg said with a gasp. "Cool idea."

"Very cool," Carrie agreed. "We can even call it the

Detective Club. There must be lots of mysteries around town to solve. We'll get some friends to join us—the smartest ones."

"I get to be club president," Greg demanded.

"What?" Carrie asked. "Why you?"

"I solved the first mystery; so, I get to be president."

"Now you kids be careful," Dr. Rydell warned. "I don't want you getting into trouble."

"'Course not," Greg and Carrie said in unison. Trouble? They were both grinning at just the thought of trouble.

"AUNT MIMI AND THE SWAMI"

1. Secret Messages Solution (page 44)

The next morning, Carrie called back. "I cracked it," she said breezily. "I figured the first word had to be *Mimi*. That gave me two letters. Then I found a word that was probably *will*. The most used letter in the message I guessed had to be *E*. After that it was a lot of trial and error, like playing 'Wheel of Fortune.'"

"So? What does it say?"

Carrie cleared her throat. "'MIMI WROTE ABOUT

HER UNCLE'S WILL. HE DIED LAST YEAR. SHE INHERITED MOST OF HIS ASSETS AND IS EVEN RICHER THAN WE THOUGHT. AMA.'"

Greg wrote it all down. "Wow! Wait till I show this to Aunt Mimi."

His aunt was in the living room, spraying a haze of underarm deodorant all over the mirrors. "It hides wrinkles," she said. "Makes me look younger. What do you have there?"

Greg let her read it for herself, then tried telling her the whole story. How the swami had a partner who broke into her apartment and sent messages. How they were con artists out after her money. But the more Greg explained, the more Mimi was unconvinced.

"You're wrong. This message is from Ama. When we got our headaches, Ama had to find some new way to contact me. Invisible spirit writing, that's what it is."

Greg grabbed the paper and read the last sentence aloud. "'She inherited most of his assets and is even richer than we thought.'"

Aunt Mimi smiled. "Yes, indeed. I inherited Uncle Frank's love of life, his curiosity, even his brown eyes. And I'm a richer person for it."

Greg gave up. "She doesn't believe me," he reported to Carrie a few minutes later. "What are we gonna do?"

Carrie thought for a second. "We have to find out what Swami Morishu is up to. Maybe I should come up to visit."

"Great. Aunt Mimi wants you to come and there are

plenty of bedrooms. I'll ask her to send Arthur and the taxi."

"This will be our second detective case," Carrie reminded him. "And this time I get to be president."

"AUNT MIMI AND THE SWAMI"

2. Observing the Swami Solution (page 57)

It was Greg who noticed the tile. At first he didn't realize exactly what was wrong with it. Then he got excited. "Hey. Henry must have been in a hurry to hide his disguise."

Carrie nodded. "You heard him rushing around in here."

"Right. So, maybe he made a mistake. You know, put the cubbyhole lid on backwards."

Now Carrie got excited. "What are you looking at?"

Greg walked over to the wall. "There's one piece of tile upside down." A Boy Scout knife came out of Greg's pocket. He stuck the blade beneath the tile and pried. It flipped off easily, the entire, thin square. Underneath was a natural hole, filling up the 6 inches between the panel and the real wall. "Wow! I was right."

"Wow!" Carrie was just as surprised. "He must have found it by accident, probably when he started using this dressing room. Great hiding place." She reached inside, pulling out a white turban, a black curly wig, and a beard. "Wait till we show this to Mimi." Carrie put on the wig and turban and began to dance around. "I am the great Swami Morishu."

Greg didn't laugh. "I don't know. Henry might have an explanation."

"What?" Carrie stopped dancing. "How can he explain the swami's stuff hidden in his dressing room?"

"He can say he didn't know how it got there. Or it's a costume from some other play. Aunt Mimi can believe almost anything. And once Henry knows that we know about his con game, it'll be a lot harder to stop him."

"I guess you're right," Carrie sighed. She was already returning the disguise to its cubbyhole and closing it up. "At least we know his secret now."

Greg shrugged. "Yeah. We'll just have to find some other way of putting the swami out of business."

SOLVE-IT-YOURSELF MYSTERIES   **137**

"AUNT MIMI AND THE SWAMI"

3. Canceling the Contract Solution (page 72)

Carrie tried to start from the beginning. "We knew Henry was a con artist."

Mimi wagged her finger. "Ha! You also said the swami was a con artist."

Carrie groaned. "He was. Swami Morishu and Henry Posley are the same man."

"Oh." This was news to Mimi and it took a moment for it to sink in.

Greg took over, explaining everything from the mirror signals to the disguise in Henry's dressing room. "Someone told us he was married, but we had no proof, not until we checked city records."

"Why didn't you warn me?" Aunt Mimi asked. "Why did you let me go and sign that stinking contract?"

"We tried to stop you," Carrie said. "Luckily, we had a back-up plan. We filled your fountain pen with disappearing ink."

"Disappearing?" Mimi looked down at the contract. "Nothing's disappeared. My signature is still there."

"It takes time. You'll have to stall. Tell Henry the

bank made a mistake and you'll write him a new check. In three days, you can tell him the truth. He'll take out the contract and your name won't be on it anymore."

Aunt Mimi thought this over and approved. "You saved me three million dollars." She smothered them both with big, wet kisses. "You're totally wonderful," she gushed. "And so was my first guru."

Greg was miffed. "What's a stupid guru got to do with this?"

"Everything. He told me this was a lucky pen. And he was absolutely right."

"SUMMER CAMP ALIENS"

1. The Disappearance Solution (page 86)

It wasn't easy picking out the smoking counselors since the camp discouraged them from lighting up in front of the campers. In fact, Carrie could think of only one smoker she'd actually seen. "Toady Todd. Remember? I saw the glow of his cigarette when he came to kick me out of your tent."

Greg came up with a second name. "Anna Fox."

Carrie was skeptical. "I'm in the crafts building a lot. I've never seen her smoke."

"She keeps a cigarette lighter in her pocket. It's a good bet that someone who carries a lighter around is a smoker."

Carrie had to agree. "Okay. Anyone else? Oh." She'd just thought of something. "Smokers sometimes have nicotine stains. Did you see that brown stain on the inside of Mr. Miller's middle finger? That's how most people hold cigarettes, between the index and middle fingers. He must be a heavy smoker."

The detectives wracked their brains, reviewing a mental list of counselors and one by one eliminating them. "Bill the cook hates cigarettes," Greg recalled. "Ruins your taste buds, he says. And I saw Terry in the office chewing nicotine gum. That means she quit cigarettes and is trying to stay off them. Anyone else?"

"That's it. Three. Three smokers who could've overheard us talking." Carrie shook her head. "It's hard to believe that one of them kidnapped Ping."

"You know what's even harder to believe?" Greg swallowed hard. "That one of them is an alien." Carrie punched him on the arm. "Ow. I'm serious."

"There are no aliens. Whatever you saw has some perfectly logical explanation."

"SUMMER CAMP ALIENS"

2. The Rescue Solution (page 101)

"So, who's the crooked counselor?" Ping asked.

"We should get started on your footprint cast," Carrie said and hurried across the field toward the crafts building. "I'll tell you as we go."

"We can eliminate Toady Todd," Greg said reluctantly. "If he was at the canoe races when the rain started, then he couldn't have been with McGruder at the barn."

"Very good," Carrie said. "Hello? Ms. Fox?" She rapped on the door and a second later, the hefty crafts counselor appeared, an unlit cigarette dangling from her lips. "You kids are in deep trouble."

"We didn't do it," said Carrie.

Ms. Fox grunted, then took out her pocket lighter and lit up. "I thought you'd be under tent arrest."

"Not yet. But just in case, can we have some crafts stuff to work with? We'll need plaster of Paris . . ." Carrie rattled off a list of things they needed.

Anna Fox felt sorry enough not to question any of their requests. She motioned them inside, pointed out the supplies, and watched as they carried them away.

Ping was thoughtful for a few seconds, then nodded. "Cigarette lighter."

"Right," Carrie said and explained for Greg. "The counselor in the barn used a match to light his cigarette. That eliminates Ms. Fox."

"Cool," Ping said. "So that leaves.... Oh." He stopped in his tracks. "The camp director, Mr. Miller. It can't be. He's such a great guy."

"And he runs the whole camp." Greg sighed. "We *are* in deep trouble."

"SUMMER CAMP ALIENS"

3. The Evidence Solution (page 114)

Carrie spread her sketch out on a table and pointed to the oak tree. "This is where Rufus dropped the bone. Your forensic people will find lots of microscopic stuff, but the big stuff was dry gravel, dry soil, dog hair, an oak leaf, and raspberry thistles."

"And that tells you where the body's buried?"

She ignored the sheriff's skeptical tone. "The dog hair doesn't help us. And the leaf probably came from when he dropped it. The raspberry thistle is interesting. Maybe Rufus pulled the bone through some raspberry bushes."

"You want us to dig under all the raspberry bushes?"

"No. We have a much better clue." She paused, trying to make it sound dramatic. "The dry soil and dry gravel"

The sheriff snorted. "Of course there's soil. And the pebbles could come from anywhere."

"Not pebbles," Carrie said. "Gravel. *Dry* gravel. Remember the downpour? The gravel and soil should have been wet, not dry."

"You're right." He gazed at the sketch. "Ah," he said and pointed at the shack. "You drew this shack on pylons. Is the floor of the shack really off the ground?"

Carrie nodded. "About eight inches. Pylons are often set in a gravel foundation. I can't see any other site that's protected from the rain. Dogs love to dig under things. And look: raspberry bushes, standing between the shack and where he dropped it."

"Uh, excuse me, Carrie. I've got a phone call to make."

Within a half-hour, the sheriff had a search warrant. A half-hour after that, his men were tearing up the shack's floorboards. They didn't have to do much digging underneath. The wolfhound had already unearthed most of the remains of Sammy Glover.

ASSISTING SHERMAN OLIVER HOLMES

INTRODUCTION

No one knew where Sherman Oliver Holmes came from or how he'd gotten his money. One day, Capital City was just your run-of-the-mill metropolitan area. The next day, a short, rotund millionaire in a deerstalker cap began showing up at crime scenes, claiming to be the great-great-grandson of Sherlock Holmes and offering his expert opinion.

Sergeant Gunther Wilson of the Major Crimes Division was irritated by how often this eccentric little man with the southern drawl would appear within minutes of a grisly murder and stick his nose into official police business. What disturbed Wilson even more was the fact that this eccentric little man was nearly always right.

"The loony should be committed," Wilson had been heard to say on more than one occasion. "He always has some outlandish theory. I'd sign the commitment papers myself—if I didn't have a soft spot for him." But Wilson didn't have a soft spot. What he did have was a phenomenal record for solving cases, thanks in large part to his "loony" friend.

To his credit, Sherman wasn't much interested in taking credit. As far as the public was concerned, the Capital City police were simply doing a better job than ever before. So Sergeant Wilson decided to swallow his pride and befriend the exasperating, unique little gentleman who had nothing better to do than pop up like a fat rabbit and do the work of an entire detective squad.

THE MISSING MONET

Sherman Holmes didn't know how he did it; but he did, and on a regular basis. Sometimes he'd see a police cruiser and stop to see what was happening. Sometimes he'd follow the sound of a siren. More often than not, he would just be walking or driving around Capital City when a sixth sense would tell him to turn here or stop there.

It was this sixth sense for crime that brought him to the Hudson Office Building on a blustery March day. Sherman settled quietly into a chair in the lobby, patiently waiting for something to happen.

The first visitor to catch his eye was a bike messenger, arriving with a package-filled backpack and a long document tube. The messenger disappeared into an express elevator labeled 31st Floor. Five minutes later, the messenger reappeared and left the building, still carrying the tube but one package lighter.

Taking his place in the elevator was an elegantly attired man, an older gentleman, using a cane as he limped heavily on his left leg.

The gentleman reappeared in the lobby ten minutes later. On his exit from the elevator he nearly collided with a woman in a Gucci suit. The umbrella in her left hand became momentarily entangled with the cane in his right.

"Watch where you're going," she snapped.

"My apologies," he replied.

The man limped off and the woman pressed her button and fidgeted with her umbrella until the elevator door closed. Her visit lasted five minutes.

Sherman was beginning to think his crime-sensing instincts were flawed. Perhaps it was this nasty cold he was just getting over. Then a pair of police officers rushed into the lobby and took the same express elevator to the 31st floor. "It's about time they called in the police," Sherman said with satisfaction.

When they left the building a half hour later, Sherman followed them to the Baker Street Coffee Shop. He slipped into the booth behind theirs, quietly ordered an English muffin, and eavesdropped.

"What was a million-dollar painting doing in the reception area?" the older cop asked his partner.

Sherman recognized him as Sergeant Gunther Wilson, an officer he'd chatted with at dozens of other crime scenes.

The 31st floor, it seems, contained the offices of the Hudson Company's top brass, and the furnishings in the reception area included a small Monet oil, about one foot square. Only three visitors had been alone there long enough to cut the painting out of its frame—a bike messenger delivering documents, the ne'er-do-well uncle of the company president wanting to borrow a few dollars, and the vice president's estranged wife, who had come to complain about her allowance. All three had visited the offices before and could have previously noticed the unguarded painting.

"Excuse me," Sherman said as he rose from his booth and ambled up to Officer Wilson and his partner.

Wilson saw the pudgy little man in his deerstalker cap and frock-coat and beamed. "Sherlock Holmes, I presume."

"That was my great-great-grandfather," Sherman answered politely. "But I did inherit a few of his modest powers. Would you like me to tell you who stole that painting?"

WHO STOLE THE PAINTING?
WHAT CLUE GAVE THE THIEF AWAY?

Solution on page 208.

A MAZE OF SUSPECTS

Sherman Holmes was out for a drive on a lonely country road. He saw the police car and the sign for the labyrinth maze at almost the same moment. "A labyrinth puzzle plus a crime," he chuckled, stepping on the brakes. "How lovely." He switched on his turn signal and pulled off into the parking lot.

The roadside attraction, "Queen Victoria's Maze," consisted of a ticket booth, a small, shabby office, and

the maze itself, a seven-foot-high square of ill-kept hedges. Curious motorists were lured into paying three dollars apiece to get lost in the confusing pathways inside the hedges.

Sherman bypassed the empty ticket booth and wandered up a gravel path and into the maze itself. Two right turns brought him to a dead end—a dead end complete with a corpse. A highway patrolman was standing over the corpse of a casually dressed man, a knife stuck between his ribs. Three men and a woman faced the officer.

"My husband Kyle and I came into the maze and split up just for fun," the woman said between sobs. "After several minutes of wandering, I wound up outside at another entrance. I was going to try again. I called Kyle, to see how he was doing. That's when I heard it—some scuffling—like a fight. Then Kyle screamed."

"I heard the scream, too," said the tallest man. "I was on a bench at the center of the maze. I didn't hear any scuffling, probably because the fountain there drowned it out. I'm Bill McQuire. I hurried out of the maze and found Mrs. Turner. The two of us went back in and discovered the body together."

"I'm the owner," said a short, disheveled man.
"Paul Moran. These people were the only three
customers in there. After taking the Turners' money at

the ticket booth, I went into the office. Abe, my electrician, was rewiring the system. I switched off the main fuse box for him. Then I walked around picking up trash. Abe was still working when I heard a man's scream."

Abe, the electrician, was the last to speak. "What Paul said is true. I was in a crawl space under the office the whole time, doing the wiring. I didn't see anything or hear anyone until the scream."

The officer bent down to examine the body. "No wallet. Maybe it was a botched robbery. But we'll have to wait for the experts."

"I'm an expert," came a voice from behind. They turned around to find a short, owlish man with a briar pipe between his teeth. "Sherman Holmes, at your service. The solution is elementary, if you'd care to listen."

WHO KILLED KYLE TURNER?
HOW DID SHERMAN DEDUCE THE TRUTH?

Solution on page 209.

BUS STATION BOMBER

"Where have you been?" Sergeant Wilson stepped around the burned and mangled debris of what had been the rear wall of the Capital City bus terminal. "I thought you must be sick."

Gunther Wilson was secretly dependent on Sherman Holmes's habit of showing up uninvited at crime scenes. He certainly wasn't used to waiting three hours for the odd, pudgy millionaire to make an appearance.

"Sorry, old man." Sherman sniffled. "I haven't been myself. Spring allergies."

Wilson pointed to a four-man squad arranging charred bits of metal on a white sheet. "The bomb was in a locker. It went off at three P.M. There were a few injuries, but nothing serious. The mechanism was an old wind-up clock wired to two sticks of dynamite. It was triggered by the alarm mechanism hitting the '3'."

"Do you have a motive?"

"Not a clue. My guess is he did it for the thrill, like some of the sick arsonists we've dealt with lately."

"Let's hope we catch him before he tries again."

Sherman glanced around the terminal. "Did anyone see who used the locker?"

"I got in touch with the night clerk." Wilson waved over a slight, sleepy-looking man. "Mr. Pollard, tell my associate what you saw."

"Certainly." Andy Pollard adjusted his thick eyeglasses and cleared his throat. "Last night as I was coming in to work, around two A.M., I saw this cab driver parking out front. He walked in with a red travel bag and put it in that locker."

Wilson waved again and two more men crossed to join them. "We checked with the cab companies. Only two taxis were in the area around two A.M. Unfortunately, Mr. Pollard can't identify the driver."

"I remember the red bag," Pollard apologized, "but not the guy's face."

The first driver was a tall, fair-haired lad, barely out of high school.

"I've been driving for about a month," he explained. "I picked up a passenger at the airport and dropped her off at the hotel on the corner. That was around two. Then I filled up at the gas station on Highland and ended my shift. If this guy says I came in here, he's lying. I haven't been in a bus station in years."

The second driver was around the same height but middle-aged and with a pronounced gut hanging over his belt. "I dropped off a fare in front of the terminal," he told them. "My fare said he'd left his car in the parking lot earlier in the day and had to pick it up. That was a few minutes after two.

"Then my dispatcher sent me to a bar on Fifth to pick up a drunk. No one was there. A man waved me down and I took him to an all-night diner on Swann Street. It's all in my log book if you don't believe me."

One of the members of the bomb squad was standing by, waiting for a chance to speak. "Excuse me, Sarge," he said. "The container was a red bag, just like the witness said. A red leather satchel."

"Thanks," Wilson said, then turned to Sherman and shrugged. "Not much to go on, huh?"

"Just enough to give us the bomber," Sherman purred. "I can't tell you why he did it, but I can certainly tell you who."

WHO BOMBED THE BUS STATION?
WHAT FACT CLUED SHERMAN IN?

Solution on page 210.

THE POSTMAN RINGS ONCE

Sergeant Wilson found the letter and envelope torn up and crammed into the bottom of a wastebasket. Reassembling it while wearing plastic gloves proved difficult.

"It's from Henry Liggit's lawyer," he finally said, looking up from the jigsaw-like puzzle. "It outlines Mr. Liggit's proposed new will, disinheriting his three nephews and leaving everything to charity."

Sherman stood behind the sergeant, peering over his shoulder. "What do you think?" Wilson asked him.

"Hmm. It doesn't take a Sherman Holmes," said Sherman Holmes, "to suspect that Mr. Liggit's suicide wasn't really a suicide."

"My thoughts exactly," the officer agreed.

Sherman and the sergeant were in Henry Liggit's library, just yards from where the millionaire lay slumped in his chair with a gun in his hand and a hole in his head.

"Our first job, my dear Wilson, will be determining which devoted nephew opened Liggit's mail and discovered the threat to his inheritance." With that, Sherman led the way into the front hall where the nervous nephews stood waiting.

All three nephews lived in the Liggit house; all three had been at home at the time of the shot. None, or so they swore, had the least idea Uncle Henry had been about to cut them out of his will.

"Uncle Henry had been depressed," said Nigel, the eldest, in mournful tones. He was sipping a martini and Sherman suspected it wasn't his first of the day. "I spent all afternoon at home. About three P.M. I walked into the front hall. I was checking the mail on that side table when I heard the gunshot."

Sherman observed a few pieces of mail on the table. "When did the mail arrive, my good fellows?"

Gerald, the youngest nephew, raised his hand. "When I got home around 2:30, the mail was already on the hall floor. I walked right across it before noticing. I picked it up and put it on the hall table."

"Did you check through it?"

Gerald nodded. "Yes, but there was nothing for me. I went straight out to the garden and sat by the pool. I, too, heard the gunshot. Around three, as Nigel said."

"I looked through the mail," volunteered the middle nephew, Thomas. "I'd just got home from a trip. I put my bags down in the hall, sorted through, and found a letter for me. I put it in my pocket, then went up to my room."

"What time was this?"

"Ten minutes to three, or thereabouts. I was unpacking when I heard the shot."

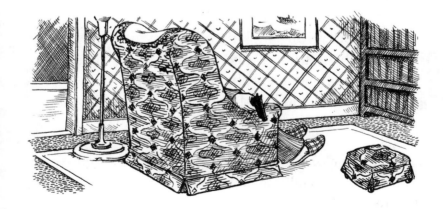

"Is the letter still in your pocket?"

With some hesitation, Thomas reached into his jacket and produced the unopened envelope. Sherman noticed a faint shoe print, a water ring, and a curious return address. "It's from a bill collector," Thomas confessed. "I've got a cash flow problem."

"Can anyone verify your arrival at the house at 2:50?"

"I can," said Gerald. "You can see the driveway from poolside. Thomas's car pulled in about ten minutes before poor Uncle killed himself."

"Yes," said Sherman. "We'll talk about suicide in a minute. Did any of you notice a letter addressed to your uncle from his lawyer?"

The nephews all shook their heads.

"Then that settles it," said Sherman. "One of you is lying. One of you knew about your uncle's plans to change his will and killed him before he could do it."

"I don't know what you're talking about," said Nigel.

"Join the club," laughed Sergeant Wilson. "I don't know what he's talking about half the time, either. But he's usually right."

WHO KILLED HENRY LIGGIT?

WHAT PROOF DOES SHERMAN HAVE?

Solution on page 211.

FOUL BALL BURGLARY

Sherman Holmes sat on a park bench, watching as the neighborhood boys played a pick-up game of baseball. "I should retrieve my great-great-grandfather's bat and teach those lads the art of cricket," the amateur detective thought, then realized he didn't know how to play it himself.

"Oh, well," he sighed. "The lads are awfully close to those houses." And that, of course, was the exact moment when the batter hit a long fly in just that direction. Glass shattered and a home alarm began to wail.

The left fielder, a boy called Jake, went after the ball. He scrambled up a high wooden fence and straddled the top, gazing at the house and yard below. "The ball broke a window, all right," he shouted back to the others. Then his eyes widened. "Hey—you better call the police. I think there's been a robbery."

The game broke up immediately. Jake lowered himself into the backyard while the other boys circled around to the front of the house and awaited the police.

Jake unlocked the door from inside and let the officers in. Sherman sneaked in right behind. The rotund little Southerner was safely ensconced behind a potted palm when a man and a woman drove up in separate cars.

The newcomers joined the police inside. Sherman edged his potted palm into a good viewing position and managed to piece together the essentials.

The newcomers were brother and sister, Larry and Laura Conners. The house had belonged to their late

father, who kept his coin collection on display on a table by the rear garden window. This was what Jake must have seen from the fence. The heavy table lay on its side, not far from the wayward baseball. Remnants of the broken window were everywhere. A patrolman

walked across the fallen tablecloth and Sherman could hear the muted crunch of glass under the white linen.

The Conners both had keys and both knew the alarm code. They had been here together just this morning, arguing about the coins.

"Laura must've come back and stolen them," snarled Larry. "Then she overturned the table in some pathetic attempt to blame it on a burglar. I was at home, ten miles from here, washing my car. My neighbors saw me. I was there right up until you called me."

Laura glared at her brother. "I was at home, too, eight miles in the other direction. I was on the phone with Aunt Doreen and doing my laundry. You can check with her if you want to."

Sherman wanted to jump out from behind the palm and instantly solve the case. But that might seem a little odd. So he restrained himself and waited until the officers were leaving.

WHO STOLE THE COINS?
WHAT CLUE POINTS TO THE THIEF?

Solution on page 212.

THE UNSAFE SAFE HOUSE

For all the help Sherman Holmes provided the police, he received little if any recognition. In fact, the officers he helped the most were often the first to make fun of his quirky personality. "They don't want people thinking some amateur is solving their cases," Sherman would say with a generous shrug. "I just wish I didn't have to sneak around eavesdropping all the time."

One of Sherman's most extreme eavesdropping cases involved hiding behind a coatrack for over an hour. On that day, his instincts for crime led him beyond a yellow-tape barricade and into the front hall of a police safe house, a normal-looking home in a modest, pleasant-looking row house in which a mob witness had just been murdered.

From behind the safety of the coats, Sherman watched as a nervous rookie stood over the body of the strangled man. A minute later, Captain Loeb strode in, his baggy suit flapping in the breeze.

"I was here protecting the witness," stammered the rookie. "Then I got a call from your office, ordering me back to the station. I left him alone. By the time I figured out the call was a fake and rushed back here, Frankie was dead."

The captain remained calm. "Who all has keys to the front door?"

"Just me," answered the rookie. "The door locked automatically behind me. I told Frankie not to open up to anyone."

Captain Loeb examined the body. "Strangled from behind, meaning he probably trusted his assailant. Who would Frankie open the door for? Let's get them in here."

The first suspect to be brought in was Lou, the victim's brother-in-law. "Frankie sneaked a telephone call to me last night at work," Lou said, staring down at the corpse. "I'm a phone company operator. Frankie didn't tell me where he was. My wife is going to go nuts when she hears."

The second suspect was Barry Aiello, the secret mob informant who had talked Frankie into testifying. "I feel like I'm responsible," he sighed. "The mob was using all their contacts to find him." Barry bent down and examined the welts around the victim's neck.

"Looks like a belt was used. Poor Frankie shouldn't have turned his back."

Captain Loeb had them both taken in for questioning, then crossed to the rack and grabbed his trench coat. "The commissioner's gonna have my head, but I suppose I gotta call him." Loeb had just pulled a notepad from his coat pocket when he saw a face staring out from behind Frankie's leather jacket. "Who in blazes are you?"

"Hi!" Sherman was so nervous, he momentarily forgot his English accent. "I'm so sorry. I know I'm trespassing, but..." He could think of only one way to redeem himself, and that was to hand them Frankie's killer.

WHO KILLED FRANKIE?

WHAT TIPPED SHERMAN OFF?

Solution on page 214.

THE CRYSTAL VANISHES

Luther brought a new pot of coffee into the dining room and began refreshing everyone's cup. "Agatha, is that the crystal ball you were telling us about?"

"Isn't it gorgeous!" The young woman in the flowing robe held it up for all to see, a round piece of cut crystal, not much larger than a baseball. "The salesman guaranteed me that it once belonged to Morgan LeFay. And this wasn't her everyday crystal either. It was her special one." Agatha passed the ball to Sherman Holmes.

"It's blooming lovely," Sherman said, managing to keep a straight face. He enjoyed his weekly dinners with Luther, Agatha, and Grimelda. The warlock and two witches might seem a little extreme to Sherman's other friends, but they were full of life and always interesting. And they accepted without question Sherman's own idiosyncrasies.

All three examined the ball, then watched as Agatha returned it to the red velvet box. "They say it has a mind of its own. If the crystal doesn't like its current owner, it will find a new one. We get along quite swimmingly, I'm glad to say."

The evening was almost over. Agatha helped
Luther, the host, clear the dining room table, while
Grimelda went to the bathroom and Sherman
browsed through Luther's library. When he returned
to the living room, Grimelda was adjusting her shawl
and checking her makeup in the mirror over the
mantle. She had always been the most attractive
witch in the coven. Sherman had heard from Luther
that there was some tension between her and the
younger, newer arrival, Agatha.

"Next week at my abode," Sherman reminded her.

Grimelda seemed startled. "Oh, that's right. We're
going to help you contact Dr. Watson. We never had
much luck contacting your great-great-grandfather, did
we?"

"We'll have to keep trying. Luther!" he shouted to
the next room. "A scrumptious dinner." Then he saw
the velvet box on the sideboard beside the full pot of
coffee. "Agatha, don't forget your crystal." Sherman
picked up the box and could instantly tell it was too
light.

"It's gone," Agatha cried when she discovered the

empty box. "Morgan's crystal has left me. I feel so rejected!"

"Oh, that's too bad," Grimelda commiserated. Luther agreed. The three witches seemed quite willing to accept the crystal's disappearance as a natural phenomenon. But Sherman knew better.

WHO TOOK THE CRYSTAL BALL?
WHERE IS IT HIDDEN?

Solution on page 215.

THE POINTING CORPSE

When the detective business was slow, the great
Sherlock Holmes had spent the long, empty hours
playing the violin. Sherman Holmes did the same, but
with less soothing results. "Maybe I should take
lessons," he would think as he sawed back and forth
across the strings. When things got really slow,
Sherman switched on one of his police band radios.

After two boring days of drizzle and inactivity, the
detective intercepted a call reporting a murder victim

found in a car. Sherman happened to be driving his classic Bentley at the time and made a quick turn up High Canyon Road.

He arrived to find Gunther Wilson standing between his patrol car and a white sedan parked beside a

panoramic view. The sergeant actually looked glad to see him. "I'm a little out of my depth on this one," he said. "It's a celebrity, Mervin Hightower. Shot at close range. I'm waiting for forensics and a tow truck. On top of being murdered, his car battery's dead."

The whole city knew Mervin Hightower, a newspaper columnist who specialized in scandalous exposés. Sherman walked around to the driver's side. An arm extended out the partially open window, propped up on the glass edge. The hand was made into a fist, except for the index finger, which was straight and firm with rigor mortis.

"He appears to be pointing," Sherman deduced. "How long has the fellow been dead?"

"What do I look like, a clock? The forensics boys will narrow it down. I saw the car and stopped to see if he needed help, which he doesn't. I recognized him, even with the blood."

Sherman looked in to see the columnist's familiar face contorted and frozen in agony. "I presume the man survived for a minute after the attack. What do you think he was pointing at, old bean? Something that could identify his killer?" Sherman lined up his eyes along the extended arm. "What story was he working on?"

Wilson pulled a newspaper from his back pocket. "Here. In today's column, he says he's going to expose some embezzlement from the City Charity Board."

"There are only three people on the Charity Board," Sherman said, checking the column for their names. "Marilyn Lake, Arthur Curtis, and Tony Pine." Then he examined the view: a glistening lake, a neon sign for Curtis Furniture and a majestic grove of evergreens. "Zounds!"

"Zounds is right. If Mervin was trying to point out his killer, he did a lousy job."

"Not necessarily." Sherman was thinking. "I think he did just fine."

WHO KILLED MERVIN HIGHTOWER?

HOW DID SHERMAN KNOW?

Solution on page 216.

BELL, BOOKE, OR KENDAL?

"My regrets, Wilson. I have no idea who killed him."

"What?" Sergeant Wilson thought he would never hear Sherman Holmes say those words. He wasn't too happy about it, either. "Okay, okay, calm down." Wilson sounded close to panic himself. "Mr. Boren, maybe you should review the facts."

Sherman and the sergeant were in the downtown offices of Boren Technologies, a designer of hand-held computers. Arvin Boren sat at his desk, eyeing the professional detective and the eccentric amateur. "Someone's been stealing our designs. My vice president, Don Silver, and I kept the problem secret. And we narrowed the suspects down to three." He pointed out the window of his private office to where a skinny kid in shirtsleeves was stuffing yellow envelopes into a mail slot.

"That's Wally Bell, an intern from City College. He does a lot of our copying and binding, so he has access to our priority documents. The heavy-set guy sitting outside my office, that's Solly Booke, my assistant. He's sending his son to private school. I don't know where he gets the money.

"The third possibility is Inez Kendal." A young woman in a tasteful, expensive suit was tacking a newspaper article to a bulletin board right next to the elevators. "Inez is director of public relations. She has the most contact with our competitors."

Sherman nodded. "Was it Mr. Silver's idea to try to trap the traitor?"

"I'm afraid so," Boren sighed. "We're developing a new version of our Wrist 2002. Don left the plans lying conspicuously on his desk. The thief never took originals, only copies. Don planned to hide in the copy room and catch the guy. Only the guy must have caught him."

Sergeant Wilson took over the narrative. "Silver was killed in the copy room by a blow to the head. Mr. Boren and an associate found the body almost immediately. All three suspects were immediately sequestered and their possessions searched. We haven't been able to locate the plans."

Sherman took the sergeant across to the window but didn't lower his voice. "The thief couldn't afford to be caught with them. My guess is the plans got thrown down that mail slot. It's the only place they could be."

Five minutes later, Sergeant Wilson persuaded a maintenance man to open the ground-floor mail chute. There the plans were, nestled right on top of a layer of yellow envelopes. "Just as I thought," Sherman said, turning to Wilson. "Now I know the killer."

WHO KILLED DON SILVER?

HOW DID SHERMAN KNOW?

Solution on page 217.

THE WAYWARD WILL

Sherman Holmes signed his name to the will and then watched as Harmon Grove signed as the other witness. "Thanks for dropping over—again," the congenial lawyer said as he slipped the will into his briefcase. "The Fielding kids can't be witnesses because they inherit."

"Not a problem," Sherman replied. This was the fourth time he had been asked over to witness a new version of Jacob Fielding's will. "You get better now, Jake," Sherman said to the frail man propped up in bed. Jacob nodded weakly and closed his eyes.

Sherman and the lawyer walked out into the hall. "This may be the old man's last will," Harmon whispered. "I don't expect he'll last the night." Solemn-faced, Anna passed them and entered the sick room.

There were three Fielding children. As their next-door neighbor, Sherman knew them well—Anna, the nurse; Brock, now a surgeon at a local hospital; and Keith, fresh out of college. All three had moved back into the family home during their father's long, difficult illness.

Harmon deposited his briefcase on the dining room table, and walked Sherman to the door. As they entered the foyer, Anna appeared at the top of the stairs. "Mr. Grove, I think . . . I think he's dead."

The two men joined the Fielding children who had already gathered in the dead man's bedroom. Brock checked for vital signs, then gently pulled the sheet over his father's face.

Half an hour later, as the people from the funeral home were removing the body, Sherman and Harmon once more crossed through the dining room. Harmon saw his briefcase and eyed it curiously. "It's been moved," he said, then opened the leather lid. "The new will. It's gone!"

Sherman and the lawyer backtracked their movements through the bedroom, dining room, and hall, hoping to find the will somehow mislaid. Finally they had no choice but to assemble the bereaved children and treat them as suspects.

"I went downstairs once after he died," Anna claimed. "To get the number for the funeral home. I called them from the kitchen. I didn't go into the dining room, and I certainly didn't touch your briefcase."

"I went downstairs to let the funeral people in," Dr. Brock Fielding said. "I saw the briefcase but didn't touch it. I didn't even know the will was in there."

Keith sighed. "Well, I didn't go downstairs at all. After Brock declared father dead, I returned to my room to call some relatives. What do we do if we can't find the will?"

"We'll have to use his last will," Harmon explained. "It's almost exactly the same. You know how eccentric he was. All three of you still get substantial bequests. He left me the same token gift. Plus small amounts go to servants and employees."

"I can find the new will," Sherman said softly. The others all turned, a little surprised to find him still in the room. "I think I know where to look."

WHERE IS THE NEW WILL?

HOW DID SHERMAN KNOW?

Solution on page 218.

THE DOC'S LAST LUNCH

Sergeant Wilson hated stakeouts. Here he was, stuck alone in a first-floor apartment, photographing the comings and goings at the home of a suspected hit man across the street. And it was a beautiful day outside, which just made things worse.

Wilson heard the door to his own apartment building close and glanced outside to see Dr. Weber's regular Tuesday patient leaving. 11:58, he noted on his watch. Time for the elderly psychiatrist to watch his half-hour game show, and then make himself lunch. When he concentrated, Wilson could hear the TV upstairs in the doctor's living room.

At 12:35, the whistle of a teakettle announced the doctor's lunch preparations. Three minutes later, the kettle was still whistling furiously. Wilson abandoned his stakeout and hurried one flight up to see if anything was wrong.

When his knocking produced no response, Wilson walked into the unlocked apartment. The doctor lay on the kitchen floor. A fruit knife lay in his right hand. A bloody steak knife lay imbedded in his back.

Wilson did his own whistling. "Wow."

"Wow is correct, dear fellow."

The sergeant turned to find Sherman Holmes standing behind him in the doorway. "This murder just happened," Wilson gasped. "How do you do it? You're like a vulture."

"Thanks awfully," Sherman said and quickly perused the scene. The noisy teakettle sat on a low flame. On a cutting board were an open can of tuna and a sliced apple, its flesh already turned brown. The TV was on in the background. "Someone interrupted his lunch."

"That much seems clear," Wilson said. "There are two other tenants in this building who stay home during the day. Let's talk to them."

Sammy Cole, on the third floor, answered the door in his underwear. "I work nights," he said with a yawn. "I got home around 11 A.M., had a little breakfast, and went to bed." Sherman looked through to Cole's kitchen and saw a half-filled carafe sitting in the automatic coffee maker. "The floors are thick," Sammy added. "I didn't hear a thing."

Glenda Gould lived across the hall from Sammy and seemed unnerved by Dr. Weber's death. "He was my psychiatrist. I told him to get better security. With all the nut cases he treats, this sort of attack was inevitable." She twisted the ring on her finger, revealing a raw patch of skin underneath. "I'll need to find another doctor."

Wilson walked back down to the crime-scene apartment with Holmes."Naturally I know who did it," Sherman said in his unique, infuriating way. "I just need to check one thing."

WHO IS SHERMAN'S SUSPECT?
WHAT WAS THE VITAL CLUE?

Solution on page 219.

A HALLOWEEN HOMICIDE

Sherman loved Halloween. It gave him a chance to
dress up as Sherlock Holmes and still seem normal.
The pudgy detective was in his usual costume,
escorting a squadron of children down Elm Street,
when he noticed a crowd gathering in front of old Miss
Cleghorn's house. "She must be up to her usual,"
chortled Sherman. "Putting on some horrific mask and
scaring the kids at the door."

Miss Cleghorn was indeed scaring the kids, but not
intentionally. Inside the open door, Sherman could see
her frail body lying in the entry hall, wearing a

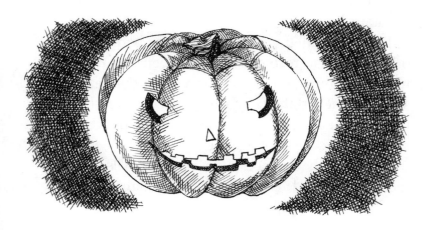

monster mask, her head surrounded by blood. A plastic bowl lay nearby, its contents of wrapped candy strewn everywhere.

Sergeant Wilson stood beside the body. He glanced over at the man with the calabash pipe and deerstalker cap. "Is that a costume, Holmes? With you it's hard to tell."

"What happened, my respectable partner in crime?"

"It's an accident. It took us a while to reconstruct what happened." Wilson pointed up to where a strand of large pearls lay centered at the top of the steps. "She was upstairs when the first trick-or-treaters rang the bell. She put on the mask and grabbed the bowl. She must have slipped on the pearls and tumbled down the stairs."

Two cars pulled up at the curb, one behind the other. Sherman recognized Miss Cleghorn's niece and nephew, Emma and Bobby, as they got out of the cars and approached the front door, both dressed for a night out and seemingly unaware of the tragedy.

"Aunt Rita," Bobby gasped.

"Your aunt had an accident," Sergeant Wilson told them. "She's dead. The kids had been coming up to the door for half an hour or so and getting no answer. One of them finally looked through the window and saw her."

Bobby noticed the spilled candy and the mask. "What's she doing wearing a mask?"

"She was obviously doing her Halloween thing," Emma said.

"She promised she wouldn't this year. We were taking her out to dinner."

"Well, obviously she changed her mind," Emma said, shaking her head. "I don't know how many times I told her not to wear a mask on the stairs."

"When did you last see your aunt?" asked Sherman.

Bobby stared at the rather overage trick-or-treater. "Uh, I dropped by this morning. My daughter left her skateboard here. Aunt Rita made me coffee and we chatted."

Sergeant Wilson grabbed Sherman by the collar and dragged him aside. "Don't try to make this a murder. The neighbors say there were no visitors since this morning."

"Someone could have driven up the back alley and come in that way," argued Sherman. "Believe me, friend, this was murder."

WHY COULDN'T IT HAVE BEEN ACCIDENTAL? WHOM DOES SHERMAN SUSPECT AND WHY?

Solution on page 220.

THE COMMERCIAL BREAK BREAK-IN

An inch of snow fell that evening, turning to a crusty sleet that hardened and made everything beautiful and treacherous. When the skies cleared, Sherman went for a stroll.

"What ho, Trent! A quiet night, eh?" Sherman waved to the uniformed guard hired to patrol the neighborhood.

"A little too quiet." Tom Trent was naturally suspicious and pessimistic, good traits for a neighborhood security guard. At the moment, he was scanning his flashlight beam across the suburban landscape. "Uh-oh." His light stopped on the side of the Warner family's home.

Sherman saw what he meant. The ladder that Bill Warner had used last fall to paint the house was now propped up against it, leading up to a second-story window. The flashlight beam scanned the rest of the house. Lights were on downstairs but not upstairs. The family had undoubtedly come home before the snowfall, since there were no footprints going up the walkway. But there were other footprints, a single set leading to the dry space under the eaves where the ladder was usually stored. The same prints led to where the ladder now stood, then retreated back to the sidewalk.

Trent checked out the ladder, stepping on the first rung and causing the wooden feet to crunch into the hardened snow. Without a word, the guard crossed to the front door, drew his revolver, and knocked. Sherman followed.

Amelia Warner answered the door. "Tom. Sherman. What's wrong?"

"Possible break-in," Trent replied, then asked a few questions. Amelia, Bill, and Frank, a visiting friend, had been home for about three hours. For the past hour, no one had gone upstairs. And no one had propped the ladder up against the house.

"Stay here," Trent ordered everyone. Then he tiptoed up the stairs and vanished around a corner. Two minutes later, he called out. "It's all clear. Come on up."

When Sherman, the Warners, and their houseguest entered the master bedroom, they found the remains of

a robbery. Drawers lay open; closets were in shambles. Bill and Amelia raced to check their valuables. Bill's wallet was gone. So were the rings and earrings from Amelia's jewelry box.

No one, it seems, had heard anything. "We were watching TV," Bill Warner said. "I went down to the basement during a commercial. I was looking for an old school yearbook to show Frank. I couldn't find it."

"I went to the kitchen for snacks and drinks," Amelia reported. "I think I went twice, during two commercial breaks."

"And I used the bathroom," said Frank. "Someone must have noticed the lights off upstairs and seen the ladder and just taken the opportunity. It wouldn't take long to grab the valuables. People always neglect to lock upstairs windows."

Amelia turned to Sherman. "You're always bragging about your great-great-grandfather. Why don't you put that genetic brilliance to a little use?"

WHO BURGLED THE BEDROOM?
HOW DID SHERMAN SOLVE THE CASE?

Solution on page 220.

AN ALARMING JEWEL HEIST

"Maybe now you'll stop bugging me," Zach Alban said as Sherman walked into his friend's shop. "See? I got that alarm system you recommended, wired straight to the police station."

"It's about time," Sherman replied. Alban Jewelers had just expanded its business and finally had some jewels worth stealing.

"Mr. Alban, I'm leaving now." Ricky Mayfield had

finished clearing out the window displays, placing the felts of precious stones into their locked drawers for the night. The door buzzed as the young assistant raced out to catch his bus.

Melanie, Alban's second in command, was putting on her jacket and looking at the newly installed alarm

panel. "Are you sure you don't want to give me the code, Zach? That way you won't always have to be here to open and close."

"Not right now. Maybe in a few days when I get more used to it."

"Whatever," Melanie said. A rumbling from the street announced the arrival of her boyfriend's motorcycle. "See you tomorrow." And she was quickly out the door, hopping onto the back of a Harley-Davidson.

Zach led the way into the back office, eager to show his friend the entire system. "Once I set the code, any broken window or open door will trigger the alarm. Twenty seconds, that's all the time I have to disarm it. Sam, why don't you go home, too?"

Sam Wells switched off the computer and wished his boss a good night. Seconds later they heard the front door buzz, signaling the last employee's departure. "Want to help me close up?" Zach asked Sherman. "I don't want to make a mistake. After your first false alarm, they start charging you a fine."

Sherman and Zach followed the instructions to the letter, then went down the block to Gil's Tavern. When they left an hour later, Sherman noticed a police patrol car parked in front of Alban Jewelers.

"Break-in and burglary," an officer informed the devastated storeowner. "The back alley window was smashed. We responded within two minutes. But the alley was empty and the crooks were already gone."

Sherman was surprised by the thoroughness of the burglary. The jewel drawers had been chiseled open and stripped of their contents. The display cases had also been broken into and ransacked, glass shards littering the hardwood floor.

"So much for my brand new alarm system," Zach said almost accusingly.

"Not so fast," Sherman said. "If it weren't for the alarm system I wouldn't know who the burglar is."

WHO ROBBED THE SHOP?

HOW DID SHERMAN KNOW?

Solution on page 221.

ALL IN THE FAMILY

Sergeant Wilson enjoyed an occasional breakfast with Sherman at the Baker Street Coffee Shop. What he didn't enjoy were the homicide calls that so often came right in the middle of the meal. He was just finishing his Belgian waffle with fruit when this morning's call took him to Gleason & Son Insurance, located on a

lonely stretch of highway. As usual, Sherman tagged along.

A uniformed officer met them in the parking lot. "The victim is Gary Lovett," the officer told them. "A Gleason & Son employee. That's Neal Gleason and his sister, Patty Lovett. She's the victim's widow." He was pointing to an anxious-looking duo, both in their late twenties. "Mr. Gleason discovered the body at about 8:30 A.M."

Neal Gleason stepped forward. His statement sounded rehearsed. "When I pulled into the parking lot, I saw Gary's car. Gary is often here early, though he's always gone before noon. If Gary wasn't Patty's husband, Dad would've fired him long ago. The front door was open. Right inside the door I saw him, like that."

Wilson examined the body in the doorway. The man's head was a bloody mess, and it took the sergeant a while to realize that the rifle now bagged as evidence had been used as a blunt instrument, its wooden stock having been slammed into his head like a baseball bat. The body was cold and rigor mortis had already come and gone.

"That's my husband's rifle," volunteered the widow.

"He kept it here at the office. Last night at home, Gary got this phone call. He said he had to go to the office and that I should just go to bed. I thought he might be going to see another woman. This morning when I woke up he was still gone. So I went to find him. I must have arrived here just a minute after my brother did."

"I think we should probably call Dad," Neal said.

That call wouldn't be necessary, for at that exact moment, George Gleason was pulling into the parking lot. The burly insurance broker eased himself out of his Cadillac and wordlessly took in the scene, the body, the bagged rifle, and his two children.

Patty ran up to him. "Someone murdered Gary," she moaned. "The police suspect us, Neal and me."

Gleason hugged his daughter, exchanged glances with his son, then turned to face Sergeant Wilson. "I killed him," he said softly and simply. "I met him here last night and shot him, right in the head. My kids had nothing to do with it."

As the uniformed cop took Gleason's statement, Wilson stepped off to the side with Sherman. "You don't have to tell me," Wilson whispered. "I picked up on the clue, too."

"Perhaps, old man," Sherman said with a smile. "But did you pick up on the right clue?"

WHO KILLED GARY LOVETT?
WHAT CLUE POINTS TO THE KILLER?

Solution on page 222.

THE LOST ETRUSCAN FIND

Sergeant Gunther Wilson rolled the library ladder over the shards of glass and water, then climbed to the top rung. "This skylight must be how the thief got in," he said, pointing to the smashed skylight and the rope dangling down into the room from a crossbeam. "Forensics can use this ladder to dust for prints."

"There won't be any prints," said a familiar, high-pitched voice. The sergeant gazed down to see Sherman Holmes standing below him in the university's research library.

"What're you doing here?" Wilson barked.

"The victim asked me to help out."

Sherman, it turned out, was a friend of Professor Plotny, the man who had acquired the small Etruscan statue that had just been stolen.

"I spent a fortune of my own money on that statuette." The burly professor wrung his hands. "I left it on the center table when I exited the building last night. I locked the door. But, of course, anyone up on the roof could have looked in and seen it."

Sergeant Wilson shook his head. "No thief goes

around rooftops with a rope, just hoping someone left valuables on a table. It had to be someone who knew the statuette and knew your rather careless habits."

A small, wiry man stepped forward, brandishing an authentic English accent Sherman would have killed for. "Next to no one knew about the statue, officer. I'm Donald Westbank, an Etruscan expert. I arrived yesterday from London. Dr. Plotny and I examined the statue together and, frankly, I was thrilled. What a find! I was a little jet-lagged, so I left the library around six, just in time for that little storm you had. I took a cab to the hotel and ordered from room service. When I got here this morning, I found Gina, the professor's assistant, unlocking the doors."

Gina, an athletic-looking graduate student, came forward with her story. "I left Professor Plotny and Mr. Westbank here yesterday at 5:30 P.M. My dorm room is just around the block. I did some studying until seven, when the rain stopped. Then I joined a friend at the Cathay Café for Chinese food. I got back to my room around 8:30."

"And your dorm building is on the other side of this block?" Wilson asked. "Are the roofs all connected?"

"How would I know if the roofs are connected?" she said. "And I resent your implication."

"So do I," the professor added. "It must have been an outsider. If you want to know my whereabouts...I left the library around 7:15 to drive to my brother's for a birthday party. I spent the night with him and his family and was the last one to get back here this morning."

Sergeant Wilson took Sherman Holmes aside. "I'm in the dark," he whispered. "But I know you've got it all figured out."

"As a matter of fact, no," Sherman lied. "I haven't a clue."

WHO STOLE THE STATUE?

WHAT CLUE POINTS TO THE THIEF?

Solution on page 223.

SOLUTIONS

The Missing Monet (page 146)

"All three suspects had receptacles that could hold a rolled-up painting." Sherman was doing his best to make his Alabama-born accent sound British. "The messenger had a document tube, old boy. The uncle had a cane. The woman had an umbrella. And while it's tempting to accuse the last person to walk through the reception area, that wouldn't be cricket. The painting could have been cut out of its frame at any time and no one may have noticed."

Wilson snickered. "So it could be any of them."

"And it could be an employee who found someplace clever to hide the painting. But only one suspect arrived limping on one leg and departed limping on the other. I think if you examine the older gentleman's cane you'll find that it's hollow."

"You may be right," the sergeant said. "We'll check it out. But let me fill you in on something, old boy. You're no relation to Sherlock Holmes. Sherlock Holmes was fictional."

Sherman laughed. "Nonsense. Why would Dr. Watson make up those stories if they weren't true?"

"Because Dr. Watson was also fict . . . Oh, forget it."

A Maze of Suspects (page 151)

The audience of five squirmed in the narrow corner of the hedge until they were all facing the strange little man with the funny accent. "Two of your stories agree on one point. The electricity was turned off—from shortly after Mr. and Mrs. Turner's arrival until after the murder."

The highway patrolman laughed. "It doesn't take a Sherlock Holmes to figure that out."

"Sherman Holmes," the little man corrected the patrolman. "And as I said, the solution is elementary. Since the fountain in the center of the maze works by electricity, it couldn't have been running at the time of the murder, as Mr. McQuire testified. Of course, Mr. McQuire didn't know the fountain was off, because he was somewhere else at the time—robbing and killing Kyle Turner, I presume."

Bus Station Bomber (page 155)

The two cab drivers, the clerk, and the bomb squad officer all gaped in disbelief.

Sergeant Wilson tried to look nonchalant. "I caught the clue, too," he lied. "But I'll let you have the fun of telling them."

"Thanks," Sherman said, playing along. "If the perpetrator had picked a more complex bomb, it wouldn't have been so easy."

"But that's what makes it hard," the bomb squad officer objected. "You can buy a wind-up clock just about anywhere. And as for the sticks of dynamite..."

"Let's stick with the clock," interrupted Sherman. "The alarm hand is what set off the explosives, correct?"

"Correct."

"So, let's say it's two A.M. and I set the alarm for three. When will the bomb go off? At three A.M.—or at three P.M. the next day?"

"At three A.M., of course, an hour later."

"Then how do you explain the fact that the bomb didn't go off until thirteen hours after the witness saw it placed inside the locker?"

The bomb expert scratched his head. "I can't explain it."

"That's right," Sherman said. "There's no way to explain it, except to say that the night clerk is lying. He planted the bomb himself—at some time after three A.M."

The Postman Rings Once (page 159)

"If it wasn't suicide," said Thomas, "then any one of us could have killed him. No one has a good alibi."

"True," Wilson agreed and turned to Sherman Holmes.

"True," Sherman agreed. "But..." And he raised a pudgy finger. "Only one of you lied about when you checked the mail." He lowered the finger, pointing it at Nigel Liggit. "You, Nigel, actually entered the front hall between 2:30 and 2:50. You steamed open the letter and read its frightening contents. You got rid of the letter—a bad job, I must say—then loaded your uncle's gun and tracked him down."

"Bravo," Nigel said with a sneer. "But you could make up a similar story about either one of my brothers."

Sherman smiled. "Let's see Thomas's letter from that bill collector." Thomas pulled it from his pocket and handed it over. "Notice the shoe print?"

"That's mine," said Gerald, "from when I came in and stepped on the mail."

"And the water ring? Where did that come from?"

"Not from me," said Thomas. "My hands were full of luggage. I went right upstairs and unpacked."

Sherman turned to face Nigel and his incriminating martini. "When you checked the mail, you put your glass on top of Thomas's letter. That means you didn't check it at three P.M., but earlier—between the time of Gerald's shoe print and Thomas's removal of the bill collector's letter."

Foul Ball Burglary (page 164)

"Excuse me," a high-pitched voice drawled. "I can tell you who stole the coins—if you're interested."

The startled officers turned to see a dapper little man step out from behind the leafy palm fronds. "Who are you?" the tall one demanded.

"Sherman Holmes, at your service. The thief was Jake."

"Jake?" The tall officer had to think for a second. "You mean the kid who discovered the robbery? How could he be the robber?"

Sherman knew he had their attention. He took his time, reaching into his coat pocket and pulling out a briar pipe.

"What young Jake discovered," Sherman said as he sucked on the unlit pipe, "was a broken window, a screeching burglar alarm, and a coin collection lying temptingly on the table. All he had to do was yell back that there'd been a robbery. Then, while the rest of us went around to the front of the house, Jake slipped inside, turned over the table, and took the coins. They may be in his pockets or he may have hidden them somewhere. But Jake's your thief."

The tall officer still looked interested. "Can you prove what you just said?"

"Of course, old bean," Sherman said, insulted at the notion that he would form a theory without proof. "Go back to the crime scene and check the broken window glass. It's underneath the tablecloth. That means the table was overturned after the baseball broke the window, not before. It couldn't be anyone but Jake."

The Unsafe Safe House (page 168)

"The name is Sherman Holmes, private investigator."
He took a deep breath then turned to the rookie.
"Please arrest Captain Loeb."

"What?" Loeb was instantly furious. "That's garbage.
I'll have your P.I. license revoked so fast..."

For once Sherman was glad he didn't have a license.
"Ask the captain how he could have arrived without a
coat and yet was planning to leave with one. And don't
let him say it's not his coat. His notepad was in the
pocket."

The rookie's hand shook as he pulled his service
revolver. "Are you sure, mister?"

"I am," Sherman replied. "I've been staring at that
bloody trench coat for an hour. Frankie would
naturally open the door to the captain in charge of his
case. Loeb took off his coat, made himself
comfortable, then strangled Frankie with his belt. It
was only after leaving the house, with the front door
locked behind him, that the captain realized he'd left
his coat inside."

The Crystal Vanishes (page 171)

"The crystal didn't abandon you," Sherman said. "It's just playing a little joke." He had to handle this delicately. The last thing he wanted was to put an end to these weekly events, something that would surely happen if one of his spirit-loving friends were exposed as a thief.

"If memory serves, Luther freshened our coffee just a few minutes ago. And yet the coffee carafe still seems to be full." Sherman carried the glass carafe into the kitchen and carefully emptied the contents into the sink. Sitting there in the bottom of the carafe was the crystal ball. "You see? It dematerialized from the box and rematerialized here."

Agatha and Grimelda laughed with relief. So did Luther, although Sherman caught his eye and gave him a serious, warning glance, letting Luther know that he knew the truth. While clearing the table, Luther had sneaked the crystal out of the box and into the carafe. As the host, he could have easily recovered it after the others had left.

The Pointing Corpse (page 175)

Sergeant Wilson scratched his head. "There's no way you can know what he was pointing at."

"Oh, yes, there is," Sherman said. "His battery's dead."

"So what?"

"So, a dead battery probably means his lights were on." Sherman checked the dashboard and saw that he was right. "Let's say Mervin had a rendezvous here last night with someone from the Charity Board, perhaps to get information for his story. That person realized Mervin was getting too close to the truth and killed him. But before dying, Mervin saw something…"

"Yeah, yeah," Wilson growled. "And he pointed to it. But which of the three things was he pointing at?"

"It was night, remember? The lake and trees would have been invisible in the dark, especially with all the cloud cover we've had lately. The one visible thing would have been that glowing neon sign. That's what Mervin meant. The killer was Arthur Curtis."

Bell, Booke, or Kendal? (page 179)

"It was the intern," Wilson guessed.

Sherman looked surprised. "No, of course not. There was no thief."

"Sure there was. Mr. Boren told us . . ." The sergeant's eyes widened. "Oh!"

"Precisely. I don't know why Arvin Boren wanted to kill his vice president, but it had nothing to do with stolen plans. He killed Silver in the copy room, then he found a witness and 'discovered' the body. Boren made up that story about Silver trying to catch the thief and, of course, Silver wasn't around to contradict him."

"What made you suspect Boren?"

"I suspected from the beginning, but I had no proof. So I made up a story about the plans having to be in the mail chute. Boren needed to preserve the illusion of a thief, so he grabbed a set of plans and tossed them down the chute. That's the only way to explain why the plans are on top of the yellow envelopes instead of underneath them."

The Wayward Will (page 182)

Sherman edged his considerable bulk between
Harmon Grove and the briefcase. Then, like a
quarterback, he tucked the leather briefcase under his
arm and lurched around to the far side of the table.
"The will is in here."

"You're crazy," Harmon shouted. "Don't open that.
It's private."

Sherman was already rummaging through the
miscellaneous files and papers. "Ah, what do you
know! Here it is!" And with a flourish, Sherman pulled
out the signed document.

"I don't know why Jacob cut you out of his will,
Harmon, old man. Had he lived another week, he
might have put you back in. It must have seemed very
arbitrary and unjust. So, you just pretended the will
was missing."

Anna's mouth was agape. "How do you know that?"

"Harmon said he was in the new will, but that
couldn't be true. Harmon, you see, signed as a witness.
And, as he himself told me, you can't witness a will in
which you inherit."

219 ASSISTING SHERMAN OLIVER HOLMES

The Doc's Last Lunch (page 186)

Sherman went to the doctor's refrigerator and opened the freezer section. "No ice in the ice tray. Just as I suspected. That's how the doctor's last patient got the kettle not to whistle until 12:35. He filled it with ice cubes and put it on a low flame."

"You mean the killer was the patient I saw leaving?"

"Yes. This nut case, as Ms. Gould so aptly put it, was clever enough to make the crime appear to have happened later. He rigged the kettle, opened the tuna, and sliced the apple. He probably even moved the body into the kitchen."

"That's a cute theory," Wilson said. "But . . ."

"Note the oxidated flesh of the apple." Sherman pointed to the browned fruit, then to the fruit knife in the victim's hand. "If the doctor had cut the apple himself, as we're meant to believe, it couldn't have turned so brown so soon. We discovered the body just minutes after he supposedly cut it."

A Halloween Homicide (page 189)

"The accident was definitely staged," Sherman whispered to his friend. "Someone came in the back way, probably bringing the mask and candy, too. Miss Cleghorn was pushed down the stairs and the scene was set. You were meant to come to the exact conclusion you came to."

"Get off it," Wilson growled. "Every death isn't a murder."

"Those pearls at the top of the stairs? You try slipping on them and see if they stay in place. In a real accident, the string would break. At the very least, the pearls would have slid out from under her feet."

"Oh." Wilson took a deep breath. "I see your point."

"If I were you, I'd question Emma. We never mentioned that Miss Wilson had fallen down the stairs, and yet she instantly assumed it."

The Commercial Break Break-In (page 193)

"You don't have to get snippy," Sherman said. His feelings were hurt, but not enough to keep him from showing off. "First off, this was an inside job. When

Trent stepped on the ladder, it crunched through the snow, proving that it had never supported any weight."

Amelia Warner gasped. "You're saying it was one of us? Let me tell you, Mr. Sherman Holmes..."

Sherman scurried behind Trent, as if looking for protection. And then, in a split second, he pulled the revolver from the guard's holster.

Sherman trained the gun on the startled guard. "It couldn't have been someone from inside the house because there were no snowy footprints leading to the door. So whoever put up the ladder didn't come out of the house or go back into it. If you'll check Mr. Trent's coat pockets, I believe you'll find the jewelry and cash."

"Me?" Trent bristled. "I'm the one who discovered the ladder."

"After you planted it there. While we thought you were so bravely searching the upstairs rooms, you were actually robbing them."

An Alarming Jewel Heist (page 197)

"The alarm didn't catch anyone." Zach still sounded angry.

"Yes, it did. Tell me, Zach. How long do you think the thief took to clean you out?"

Zach glanced around the showroom. "A minimum of five minutes, probably ten."

"And yet, when the police got here two minutes after the alarm, the burglar was already gone."

"Yeah." Zach scratched his head. "That's impossible."

"Not if the burglar was already inside. After we left, he came out of hiding and took what he wanted. He set off the alarm when he left the shop, not when he arrived."

"You say he. It was a man?"

"It was Sam Wells. He was the only person we didn't actually see exiting the shop. He must have hidden in a closet or behind a counter until after we left. It had to be him. No one else could have come in while we were still here, not without setting off the door buzzer."

All in the Family (page 201)

"George Gleason didn't have a chance to ask any questions," Wilson explained confidently. "He saw the victim's bloody head and the rifle and assumed Lovett had been shot. But, of course, he hadn't been."

"And that indicates his innocence?"

"Absolutely. He's protecting his kids."

"Which is exactly what he wants us to think."

Wilson frowned. "What are you talking about?"

"Gleason wants us to think he's making a false confession. He knew we'd pick up on his mistake and strike him off our suspect list. Very clever of him."

"How do you figure that?"

"Because he knew Lovett had been killed last night. Lovett is often here early, but he rarely stays past noon. An innocent man would have assumed Lovett had been killed this morning. Only the person who telephoned him last night and lured him here would know when Lovett had been ambushed and killed."

The Lost Etruscan Find (page 205)

"I don't believe you," Sergeant Wilson growled. "You know who did it."

It pained Sherman to lie, but he managed to swallow his pride. "On the contrary, Wilson. I'm completely stumped."

Wilson bellowed, but Sherman stuck to his story.

After Wilson and the others left, Professor Plotny

breathed a sigh of relief. "Thank you, old friend, for not giving me away."

"Well, you didn't commit any crime, other than breaking a school skylight. The statuette was a forgery, I imagine?"

"Right," the professor admitted. "I didn't discover it until yesterday with Westbank. Luckily, he was new to the piece and too jet-lagged to see it. A clever forgery, but one that could ruin my reputation. I had to get rid of it or else be made a laughingstock. What gave me away?"

Sherman pointed to the floor. "The rainwater. It means the skylight was broken before the rain stopped at seven last night. But according to your story, you didn't leave the library until 7:15."

Plotny nodded. "I used the ladder to get up the skylight and fake the break-in. The rain was just beginning to let up. I never thought it might give me away."

ASSISTING CAL Q. LEITER

THE CASE OF THE CARNIVAL PROBABILITY GAME

The smells of buttered popcorn, cotton candy, and fried dough filled the air as Midville Police Chief Arthur Smart and his partner, 12-year-old junior detective Cal Q. Leiter, passed through the gates of the 85th annual Midville Fair. The Chief had been asked to participate in the pie-eating contest, and Cal had tagged along to support him.

"You know, it's gonna be difficult to stick to my diet today," said the Chief, eyeing the food stands that lined both sides of the walkway. He stopped in front of Perry's Pizza booth. "Maybe I'll have just a tiny slice of pizza before the contest."

"Do you really think that's a good idea, Chief?"

"Give me one good reason why I shouldn't."

Before Cal could reply, the Chief blurted out, "Hey, look. That's my cousin Norman arguing with that vendor over there."

Cal looked across the way and spotted a short, pudgy man who could pass for the Chief's twin gesturing wildly and stomping up and down. The

Chief and Cal rushed over to see what the commotion was all about.

The vendor, a lanky man with long sideburns, stood behind his counter, shaking his head smugly. "You lost, fair and square," he said, pointing at Cousin Norman.

The Chief patted Norman on the back. "Norman, what's going on here? I've never seen you this angry."

"I'll tell you what's going on here," Norman said through gritted teeth. "A big-time ripoff! This guy here is running some sort of crooked scam. I just can't figure out how he's doing it."

Cal looked up at the sign over the booth. It read: "CHANCES ARE—A GAME OF LUCK. Toss three coins. One head, you win $3. Two heads and the vendor wins. Three heads or no heads, no one wins, and we try again. Cost to play: $2."

"Let me get this straight," said the Chief. "Let's say you play once and win. It cost you $2 to play, and you won $3, so you really made $1. Isn't that right, Cal?"

Cal nodded and began drawing a diagram in his math notebook.

"And if you lose, you lose the $2 you paid to play, right?"

Again Cal nodded.

The vendor gave his side of the story. "Look," he said. "It's twice as hard to get two heads as it is to get one head. That's why it's a fair deal that if I win, I get twice as much as when I lose."

The Chief thought for a moment. "Makes sense to me."

"Wait," screamed Cousin Norman. "I've played this game 48 times. I've won 16 times, he's won 18 times; neither of us won 14 times. I've lost 20 bucks to this schemer. That shouldn't happen, should it?"

"Hey, haven't you heard of a lucky streak?" asked the vendor, smirking.

The Chief picked up the three coins from the counter and carefully examined each of them. "Nothing's wrong with the coins, Norman. Look, I'm sorry you lost, but it appears that this just wasn't your day. That's all."

"It doesn't make sense," said Norman. "Probability says I should have won twice as often as he did and that we should have broken even money-wise, doesn't it?"

Finally, Cal spoke up. "No, it doesn't," he said. "In

fact, things pretty much went according to probability."
Cal looked up at the Chief. "Chief, your cousin is not
correct about probability, but he is correct about one
thing: This game is a ripoff. Big time. This vendor has a
guaranteed winner with his game."

"Well, that's enough for me," bellowed the Chief. He
turned to the vendor. "You, sir, are shutting down and
coming downtown with us."

How is this game unfair? What did Cal figure out?
Solution on page 277.

THE CASE OF THE MAYOR'S RED OFFICE

Midville Police Chief Arthur Smart and his 12-year-old sidekick Cal Q. Leiter stood staring in shock at the mayor's office. Everything—the ceiling, the walls, the carpet, the furniture—had been slopped with bright red paint. It was an unbelievable scene.

Just then, the honorable Midville mayor, Linda Fuller, stormed into the room. "We must find out who did this," she said, turning to the Chief. "I want you to make finding this vandal your number-one priority, Chief."

"I've already got two of my best officers on this," replied the Chief.

Cal took out his trusty notebook. "When did this happen, Chief?"

"This morning between 10:30 and 11:00. The

entire staff was with the mayor at a dedication."

Suddenly, the door swung open, and two Midville police officers arrived with three people. Two of the civilians, a man and a woman, wore painting overalls which just happened to be covered with red paint. The third person, a gray-haired man in a three-piece suit, stood beside the painters, shaking his head in disbelief.

"Chief," said Officer Beth Belisle, "we have some definite leads on this case." The officer pointed to the gray-haired man and said, "This is Ned Woodland, owner of Woodland Painting. The other two are, obviously, painters. They work for Mr. Woodland."

"What's the scoop here?" asked the Chief.

Mr. Woodland spoke up. "These officers spotted my painters leaving work today and brought them in. I know they look like logical suspects because of the red paint, but they didn't do it. There's no way."

Cal was curious. "Were you with them all morning, sir?"

"Let me explain," said Mr. Woodland. "Harry and Sue here are painting rooms in a hotel downtown. The hotel has 50 identical rooms, and they've done about half of them so far. Sometimes they work alone and sometimes together. I've timed them together many times and it takes them two hours as partners to do a room. I've also timed Sue when she's done a room alone, and it consistently takes her six hours. I've never timed Harry alone."

"That doesn't answer the kid's question," said the Chief.

"O.K.," said Mr. Woodland. "I was with Sue virtually the entire morning, so I'm her alibi. I checked in on Harry at 7:00 A.M. when he was starting, and again at 11:15 when he had just finished. It takes 30 minutes to get to the mayor's office from the hotel. That's a one-hour round trip. It must have taken 10 to 15 minutes to vandalize this office. That would leave Harry three hours to paint that room back at the hotel. I don't think he's capable of doing that—it takes Harry and Sue two hours together."

The Chief frowned. "Well, we'll never know if he's capable, will we? We don't have enough information to solve the math problem."

Just then the mayor yelled, "Aha!" She pointed to Harry. "I knew you looked familiar! You used to work for our town. I fired you last year for skipping work too many times. I'll bet you did this to get revenge."

"Sorry, Mayor, that's not proof," said the Chief. "And, remember, we don't have enough math info to solve this case."

Cal held up his notebook. "Yes, Chief, we DO have enough information. Not only did Harry have motive, but he also had the time. And here's the math to prove it."

How did Cal figure that Harry had time to commit this act of vandalism? (HINT: Use the least common multiple to help you figure this out.)
Solution on page 278.

THE CASE OF THE HIT-AND-RUN TAXI DRIVER

"This is going to be a bear of a case to solve," said Midville Police Chief Arthur Smart, swabbing the perspiration from his forehead with a damp handkerchief. "We can't talk to the victim, and there were no witnesses."

"I know, Chief," said 12-year-old junior detective Cal Q. Leiter. "But you can never underestimate the power of mathematics when it comes to solving problems. As the great mathematician Pythagoras once said, 'Number is the origin of all things, and the law of number is the key that unlocks the secrets of the universe.'"

It was a hot, humid, stifling day in late August. Chief Smart and Cal were standing in front of an old brick house on Mountain Road, about three miles from Midville Center. The house was owned by a man named Peter Wheeler.

Earlier in the day Wheeler had been found unconscious on the side of the road near his driveway. He had been beaten and robbed. Wheeler had written the words "TAXI DRIVER" in the soft shoulder sand on the side of the road before he had passed out. The only other clue was a $3.90 taxi receipt for a 3.3-mile trip that police officers had found on the ground near Mr. Wheeler.

"Poor guy," said Chief Smart, as he cased the grounds for more clues. "I hope he regains consciousness soon. The doctors are hopeful that he'll come out of it in a day or so."

"By then the criminal could be long gone," said Cal.

The Chief frowned. "That's why we need to solve this case, pronto. But where do we even begin? Except for the message in the sand and the taxi receipt, we've come up empty in the clues department."

"Chief, how many taxis do we have in Midville?" asked Cal.

"Just three," answered the Chief, mopping his sweaty brow. "And I have an info report on each one, back in the cruiser."

While Chief Smart went to the patrol car to get the official report, Cal removed a math notebook from his tattered backpack. He recorded all of the facts he knew thus far.

Seconds later the Chief returned, holding a manila folder in his right hand and two bottles of water in his left. He tossed Cal one of the bottles.

"As I said, there are three taxis: Freddy's Taxi, Smalltown Taxi, and ASAP Taxi." The Chief then opened the manila folder and read off the facts from the report. "Freddy's taxi driver is Freddy Yost. He charges an initial rate of $1 for the first half-mile and then 10 cents for each additional tenth of a mile. Smalltown Taxi is driven by Mary Jill Haverhill. She charges an initial rate of $1.10 for the first half-mile and then 10 cents for each additional tenth of a mile. And ASAP Taxi is really Tony Sadowski. He charges an initial rate of $.50 for the first two-tenths of a mile and then 10 cents for each additional tenth of a mile."

The Chief looked up from the report and sighed. "I know this information should help somehow. But I don't know where we begin when it comes to working with all of these numbers." The Chief stopped talking and took a big gulp of water. "I guess we're going to have to use the old guess-and-check method and hope we stumble upon some sort of a clue."

By this time, Cal had finished writing the facts in his notebook. Working diligently, he spent the next few minutes organizing the information.

The Chief pointed to the car. "Let's go back to the office and try to—"

"Hold on, Chief," interrupted Cal. "We've got someplace we need to go first." He finished drinking his bottled water. "We have a suspect to question, a certain taxi driver who almost got away with beating and robbing a person."

"How in the world did you make sense out of all of

those numbers?" asked an astonished Chief Smart.

"By organizing the facts, Chief," answered Cal. "As I told you earlier, you have to believe in old Mr. Pythagoras. Numbers truly are the keys that unlock the secrets of the universe."

How did Cal know which taxi driver attacked Mr. Wheeler? *Solution on page 276.*

THE CASE OF THE CHIEF'S OLD PARTNER

Cal Q. Leiter looked up from his book, *The History of Irrational Numbers,* and saw Becky Smart, the Chief's daughter, standing in the doorway of Chief Smart's office.

"This is a fascinating book," said Cal. "You know, once I start reading this stuff, I can't seem to stop."

"I know, Cal; I know," said Becky. "But if you want my help with the research paper that's due tomorrow, we need to go to the library."

"Oh, all right," said Cal. He jammed the book into a tattered backpack and reached for his coat.

Suddenly, Chief Smart charged through the door. "Kids, I need your help," he said, ushering Cal and Becky out the door. "Hurry, hurry. The patrol car is parked out front."

Riding in the Chief's cruiser, Cal and Becky sat patiently, waiting for the Chief to tell them where they were going. But the Chief said nothing. He drove silently, his eyes riveted to the road.

After a few minutes had passed, Becky spoke up. "Dad, what's going on here? You come racing into your office and whisk us away, practically shoving us down the stairs and into your patrol car; and then you say absolutely nothing. What gives?"

The Chief managed a feeble smile. "I'm sorry, Beck. I guess my mind is on poor old Wally Wilkerson."

"Who?"

"My old partner, Wally Wilkerson." The Chief pointed to a faded photograph that was attached to the sun visor on the passenger's side. "Wally's in the first row, the third one from the left. He was a veteran cop when I was a rookie. Wally retired from the force about 15 years ago, and now he works as a security guard at that ritzy high-rise building over in Mercer."

"Is he in some sort of trouble?" asked Cal.

The Chief nodded. "He sure is. Two hundred thousand dollars was stolen from the security box in the vault that Wally was supposed to be guarding. Of course, everybody is furious with Wally."

When the three friends arrived at the high-rise building in Mercer, they found Mr. Wilkerson in the ground floor lobby, surrounded by a crowd of people.

"Like I told you earlier, Judkins, the elevator man, phoned me and told me there was trouble in the basement," said old Mr. Wilkerson. "When I stepped off the elevator there, I got clubbed on the head from behind."

"Oh come on, old-timer, you're just trying to cover up for falling asleep on the job," said a short, bearded man who was wearing an elevator usher's suit. "I never called you. Besides, I've seen you asleep on the job twice this past week."

Mr. Wilkerson shook his fist at the elevator operator. "Darn you, Judkins, that's a lie, and you know it."

Chief Smart wove his way through the crowd and approached Wally Wilkerson. "Come on, Wally," the Chief said calmly. "Let's go somewhere to talk."

A few minutes later, Cal, Becky, the Chief, and Mr. Wilkerson were sitting on a bench in the ground floor lobby.

"I'll stake my reputation as an ex-cop that Judkins did it," said Mr. Wilkerson. "That creep has been staking out the vault for the past two weeks and in the meantime has been trying to make me look bad whenever he's had the opportunity. I'm sure it was all part of his plan to plant in people's minds that I was an incompetent old goof and then conk me over the noggin so he could get to the vault."

Mr. Wilkerson handed the three detectives the robbery report. "Judkins says that he was working in his elevator when the money was stolen," he said, shaking his head. "But nobody remembers seeing him at the elevator that he claims to have been in."

After listening to Mr. Wilkerson, the detectives met Judkins at the elevator he operated. A slick talker, Judkins maintained that he was working his shift as elevator usher when the theft took place.

"I've got other people's statements here, Judkins," said the Chief, holding up the copy of the police report. "And no one recalls seeing you working this elevator between 9:00 and 9:15."

"That's because no one ever remembers the elevator usher." Judkins reached for a worksheet that was hanging on the elevator wall. "Take a look at this," he crowed. "I arrived at 9:00 A.M., taking my station at the ground floor. The robbery occurred at 9:10. This is a running tally of what I did during the time the robbery took place. You can clearly see that with all of this going up and down and down and up, I was busy working here in this elevator at 9:10."

The Chief grabbed the tally sheet and read the following: "+6, − 4, +5, − 8, +2, +4, −7, +2, +2, − 7, +5, +3, − 5, +3, +2, +7, − 4, + 8, − 2, −3, + 4, − 4, +9, − 8, +5." He then gave the tally sheet to Cal and Becky. "There's more, too. Certainly enough to keep Mr. Judkins busy all morning, just like he said."

"Mr. Judkins," said Becky, looking at the elevator panel which housed the control buttons. "How many floors are there in this building?"

Judkins' eyes narrowed suspiciously. "There's a basement, a ground floor, and then floors 1 through 15."

Cal fumbled for his math notebook and began calculating. After a few minutes, he was finished. He tore out the piece of paper and handed it to the Chief.

The Chief scratched his head. "What does all of this mean?"

"It means Mr. Judkins has been lying," said Cal. "He must have hurriedly written this false tally report after robbing the vault. If you look closely, you'll see that in his rush to provide an alibi, Mr. Judkins made a huge mistake."

What was Judkins' mistake? *Solution on page 277.*

THE CASE OF THE QUESTIONABLE CARPET DEALER

"After we're done at the carpet store, remind me to stop at the bakery across the street," said Police Chief Arthur Smart.

The Chief's partner, 12-year-old Cal Q. Leiter, laughed. "That's not part of your new diet, Chief," he said. "What's the matter, the garden salad you had for lunch didn't fill you up?"

"That salad wouldn't have filled up a hamster," replied the Chief. "Besides, I'm getting tired of eating salads. That's three days in a row that my wife has packed a small salad for my lunch."

The Chief steered the patrol car to the curb and parked in front of a store called The Magic Carpet. With notebook in hand, Cal hopped out of the car. The Chief, a step behind Cal, was still eyeing the bakery as the two friends approached The Magic Carpet. Just then, a tall, redheaded lady sprinted out the store's front door.

"Well, if it isn't Shady Sadee Simmons," said the Chief. "What are you doing here?"

Shady snorted. "I own this store," she said. "I'm the one who phoned in the robbery."

"Trying to make an honest living for once—eh, Shady?"

"Yes, I am," she responded. "But wouldn't you know it. In a bit of irony, I've been a victim of a crime."

The Chief eyed Shady suspiciously. "How's that?"

"Well," Shady began, "I opened this store just last week—with money I earned from an investment—and I was robbed this morning."

The Chief rolled his eyes. "Right, Shady, an investment. That's a funny one."

"I've turned over a new leaf, Chief," she said. "And stop calling me Shady."

Cal spoke up. "Could you tell us what happened, Ms. Simmons?"

Shady smiled. "Yes, young man, I can," she said. "I had five of my best area rugs stolen. They were handmade, highly crafted products worth $1000 each."

"Where were they stolen from?" asked Cal.

Shady gestured to the store. "Out back, in the warehouse." She started toward the door. "Come on, I'll take you there."

Cal and the Chief followed Sadee Simmons through the store, out the back door, and into the warehouse.

Once inside the warehouse, the Chief whispered to Cal, "I don't trust her for one second. I'll bet you dollars to doughnuts that she's been up to no good."

"Maybe she has changed, Chief. Let's see what this is all about."

As Sadee talked to the Chief, Cal looked around the tiny warehouse and saw it was empty. "Where were the carpets, Ms. Simmons?"

"All five were on the floor, stretched out. I had unrolled them and set them out to be vacuumed and shampooed."

"Were all of these rugs the same size?" asked Cal.

"Yes."

The Chief cut in. "This is an awfully small warehouse, Shady—I mean, Sadee. What are the dimensions?"

"It's 40 feet by 50 feet, 2000 square feet."

Cal jotted the information in his notebook. "You said all of the rugs were the same size. What size would that be?"

"Each was 20 feet by 18 feet."

The Chief fished a calculator out of his coat pocket and did a few calculations. "20 times 18 equals 360, and 360 times 5 equals 1800. So, the five carpets have a total of 1800 square feet. That means there's plenty of room for the carpets to fit."

"Yes," said Sadee. "Your figures are correct, Chief. I had plenty of room for the carpets. In fact, there were a couple of feet between any two carpets."

"Well, Sadee, I'll put my best officers on this," said the Chief.

Cal grabbed the Chief by his coat sleeve. "Wait a second, Chief. I've just drawn a picture that you need to see. Things are not what they might seem as far as the math of this matter is concerned."

The Chief snatched the paper from Cal and took a look. "Well, I'll be," he said, shaking his head. "Look's like Sadee is still Shady after all." The Chief turned to Sadee. "Nice try, Shady. You almost pulled this one off. But it's off to police headquarters for you."

What did Cal figure out by drawing a picture?
Solution on page 280.

THE CASE OF THE MISSING COUNTRY CLUB FUNDS

It was 7:00 o'clock on Saturday morning. Young Cal Q. Leiter looked out the clubhouse window at the first tee, where a dozen or so golfers were waiting to tee off. Cal yawned and stretched. He was half asleep. The 10-minute ride from his house to the Whispering Pines Country Club had done little to wake him up.

Cal looked over at his friend, Police Chief Smart, and chuckled. The Chief was ordering coffee, doughnuts, and muffins at the clubhouse restaurant. He had told Cal that his low-fat diet was being put on hold for just this one day.

After the Chief paid for his food, a large, gray-haired man approached him, and the two walked over to where Cal was standing. The Chief spoke first. "Cal, this is Mr. Dean, president of Whispering Pines Country Club."

Cal shook Mr. Dean's hand. "Nice to meet you, sir."

Mr. Dean cleared his throat. "Well, gentlemen, we at Whispering Pines have a problem of great magnitude. I believe that our golf association treasurer, Lenny Ray, may have embezzled Whispering Pines money."

"Got any proof?" asked the Chief.

Mr. Dean frowned. "Not anything tangible," he said. "But when a man of modest income all of a sudden goes out and buys an expensive sports car and a whole new wardrobe and then tells you that the golf association funds have run dry.... Well, it gets one thinking."

"How much was in the treasury?" asked Cal.

Mr. Dean frowned again. "I don't know," he said sadly. "Lenny claimed the computer crashed after he had distributed funds to the chairpeople of the various club committees. He says he can't remember how much was in there before he distributed the money."

"Where are the chairpeople of each of those committees now?" inquired Cal.

"In the meeting room, out back," answered Mr. Dean. "I called all of them in this morning, so they could talk with you."

Cal and the Chief questioned each chairperson. When they were through, they met with Mr. Dean in his office.

"Well, that wasn't any help," said the Chief, shaking his head. "Lenny Ray told the chairpeople what fraction of the total treasury fund they were given, but without knowing how much money was in the treasury beforehand, we're at a dead end."

"Drat," Mr. Dean sighed. "Well, you gave it your best, gentlemen. Thank you for trying."

Cal looked up from his math notebook. "Hold on, Mr. Dean," he said, smiling. "I think we can help you."

"But we don't know how much money was originally in the treasury," said the Chief, looking at Cal blankly.

Cal handed his notebook to the Chief.

The Chief read the notes aloud. "Chairpersons' report of treasury budget. The treasury funds were allocated in the following manner: lawnmowing equipment ($\frac{1}{4}$); course supplies ($\frac{1}{5}$); pro shop clothes ($\frac{1}{20}$); restaurant supplies ($\frac{1}{18}$); employee salaries ($\frac{3}{10}$)."

Chief Smart scratched his head and handed the notebook back to Cal. "What does all of this tell you, Cal?"

"We can't figure out how *much* Lenny Ray embezzled," said Cal, as he finished up with his calculations. "But we can prove that he *did* embezzle. It's right there in the numbers."

How did Cal figure out that there was money missing from the treasury? *Solution on page 280.*

THE CASE OF THE GREEN PEPPER AND ONION PIZZA DECISION

"Well, Cal, what are you going to have?" asked Midville Police Chief Arthur Smart.

Cal Q. Leiter looked up from his menu and shrugged. "I don't know, Chief; everything looks great."

Cal and the Chief were sitting in a booth at Joyce's Pizza Palace with Midville mayor Linda Fuller and Midville town manager Diane Stallworth. The Chief and Cal had just wrapped up an important case, and

the mayor and town manager had invited them to lunch. The mayor said it was the town's treat.

At this moment, the smell of pizza wafted through the tiny restaurant, and Cal was getting hungrier by the second. He cleared his throat, hoping the Chief would catch the hint.

"What about you two?" the Chief asked, waving his menu toward the mayor and town manager.

"I like green pepper and onion," answered Mayor Fuller.

"Sounds good to me," echoed Town Manager Stallworth.

The Chief broke into a big grin. "That's my favorite topping, too."

"Well, let's make it unanimous," said Cal. "Green pepper and onion."

The Chief put on his reading glasses and looked at the menu. "It costs $5.50 for a 12-inch pizza and $11 for a 24-inch pizza." He paused. "Should we order four small or two large?"

"Chief, what does it mean when it says a pizza is a 12-inch or 24-inch pizza?" asked Cal.

"That's the distance...across the pizza."

"You mean the diameter, Chief?"

"Yes." The Chief nodded. "If you want to get technical, the diameter."

Cal reached for a napkin and began scribbling calculations.

Just then, the waiter approached the booth. "Have you made your decisions?"

"Everyone wants green pepper and onion pizza," said the Chief. "But we haven't decided whether we should get four 12-inch pizzas or two 24's."

"It doesn't matter," said the waiter, his voice ringing with confidence. "A 12-inch pizza costs $5.50. A 24-inch pizza costs $11. Seeing how 24 is double 12 and $11 is double $5.50, it's going to cost the same and you're going to get the same amount of pizza either way. I recommend four small, so you can each have your own pizza."

"We'll take your advice, sir," said the Chief.

"Wait just a second," said Cal, holding up the napkin. "It does make a difference whether we order two large or four small. And since the bill is the town's treat, I think we should make sure we spend the money wisely."

"What are you talking about?" said the Chief, yanking the napkin out of Cal's hand. He looked at Cal's calculations. "He's right. The kid is right again."

The Chief looked at the waiter. "We've changed our minds," he said. "We'll go with two large green pepper and onion pizzas."

"Actually, Chief, we need to order just ONE large pizza," said Cal. "With one large, we'll get the same amount as we would if we ordered four small, and we'll save the town $11."

Upon hearing that statement, the Chief, the mayor, and the town manager all turned to Cal in disbelief.

"Even though it seems impossible, it's true," said Cal. "With the diameters of these particular pizzas, one large pizza has the same area as the combined areas of four small pizzas. And I can prove it by using pi on these pizza pies."

What did Cal figure out? How can one large pie possibly be the same amount of pizza as 4 small?
Solution on page 278.

THE CASE OF THE FISHY ALIBI

Junior detective Cal Q. Leiter tried on his new baseball glove for about the zillionth time. Chief Smart had given the mitt to Cal as a token of his appreciation for the many cases that Cal had helped him solve.

"I'll bet you'll make some terrific catches now," said Chief Smart.

Cal nodded. "This will certainly help," he replied. "My old glove was falling apart, and I had been using duct tape to hold it together."

"You know, my daughter Becky is a darn good softball player," said the Chief. "And a pretty good catch, too. Ha, ha. Get it? Pretty good catch. After we solve this case, you ought to drop by and pay her a visit."

Cal blushed. He had a crush on Becky, and the Chief liked to tease him about it. "Yeah, maybe later. But we have work to do first."

Cal and the Chief were on their way to the Midville wharf. The day before at 4:00 P.M. a man had robbed Roland's Fish and Chips restaurant, a cheap eatery located on the pier. The suspect was Frank G. Roy. Cal and the Chief had an appointment to meet Mr. Roy at the site of the crime.

When Cal and the Chief arrived at the restaurant, they were greeted by the strong smell of fresh fish. The

suspect, Mr. Roy, was sitting at a table, a plate of fried shrimp in front of him.

"I'm innocent, I tell you," said Frank G. Roy. "And I have two witnesses to prove it."

"Who?" asked the Chief.

Frank pointed to two men sitting at the bar. "Those two, Malcolm Morrissette and Paddy Smith," he said. "Yesterday at 4:00, the three of us were working on Paddy's boat at a dock that's about a mile from this wharf."

Upon hearing their names, Malcolm Morrissette and Paddy Smith got up from their seats and strolled over to Roy's table.

When questioned, both men supported Frank's story. "You see, all three of us have our own boats and run our own island touring services," said Malcolm.

"Yeah," said Paddy, his lips curling up into a sarcastic grin. "When one of us needs help, the other two always come through."

"Tell us about your touring services," said Cal. He grabbed a notebook from his tattered backpack.

"Well," said Frank. "We all left the pier yesterday morning at 8 A.M. That's the time we depart each morning."

"Right," said Paddy. "I did my regular route, with each round trip being three hours."

"And I did my regular route," said Malcolm. "That's six hours each round trip."

"And mine is four hours," added Frank.

Cal jotted down the numbers in his math notebook. "Are your trips nonstop?" he asked. "In other words, as soon as you drop tourists off, do you pick up the new ones?"

"That's correct," answered Paddy. "And we are always right on schedule each time we go out. I always take exactly three hours, Malcolm six hours, and Frank four."

"We do that from 8 A.M. until 8 P.M. every day," said Frank.

"I suppose we could try to find some of the passengers these three characters had yesterday," the Chief spoke up. "Then we could find out if they really were working on a boat together at 4 P.M."

Cal smiled. "No need to do that, Chief. Frank's alibi

is all wet. They were right about one thing, though. When one of them needs help, they other two do come through—even if it means lying. These three gentlemen should be arrested."

How did Cal know they were lying? What was wrong with the alibi? *Solution on page 279.*

THE CASE OF THE REFORMED BANK ROBBER

Cal Q. Leiter and Becky Smart had just finished cleaning Chief Smart's office when the Chief burst into the room.

"Cal, I got a phone call from a parole officer named Bea Williams," said the Chief. "Evidently one of her—ah—clients is a suspect in a bank robbery that occurred yesterday afternoon in the town of Harrisonburg. I said we'd meet her at her Midville office in about ten minutes." He nodded in Becky's direction. "You can come along, too, Beck."

Cal grabbed his baseball cap and followed Becky and the Chief outside to the patrol car. "This robbery was reported on the news last night," Cal said as he slid into the back seat. "They said the robber made off with $50,000."

"Yes," the Chief said, adjusting his rear-view mirror. "And get this: Bea Williams' client specialized in robbing banks a few years back." The Chief pulled out into Main Street. "But I'm sure that's just a coincidence," he added sarcastically.

At Ms. Williams' office, Cal, Becky, and the Chief found the parole officer waiting in her conference room. Beside her sat a muscular man wearing a loud plaid sports jacket.

"This is Casey Rockleford," said Ms. Williams, pointing to the muscular man. "Casey, this is Chief Smart."

"I'm innocent," snarled Casey. "Sure, I drove Ms. Williams up to Harrisonburg early yesterday afternoon, but I was back here in Midville when that robbery took place."

"Please tell us your story from the beginning, Mr. Rockleford," said the Chief.

Casey sprang from his chair and began pacing. "It's this simple," he said. "Ms. Williams and I left Midville in her car yesterday at 2:00 in the afternoon. And we pulled into Harrisonburg at 4:00. I dropped her off, turned around, and came directly home."

Ms. Williams nodded. "Yes, that's correct. Mr. Rockleford drove me to Harrisonburg and dropped me off to stay with my sister's family. I was planning to ride back with my mother—who has been with my sister's family for the past few days—next week, but when I heard about the trouble that Mr. Rockleford might be in, I had my mother drive me home this morning."

"Ms. Williams," said Cal, "are you sure about these departure and arrival times that Mr. Rockleford has given?"

"Positive," she replied.

Rockleford stopped pacing and pointed at the Chief. "I'm telling you, Chief, I did nothing wrong yesterday."

"How fast did you drive?" asked Cal.

"With Ms. Williams in the car, I had the cruise control set at 55 miles per hour for the entire way to

Harrisonburg." Rockleford bit his lip. "On the way back, I gotta admit, I drove a little faster than that."

"He's right about the ride to Harrisonburg," said Ms. Williams, nodding. "He drove exactly at 55 mph. Of course, that car can't go much faster anyway. Before we left Midville, a mechanic told us we'd be lucky to get that old car up to 65 mph, because the transmission is starting to falter."

Cal began writing in his math notebook. "Did you spend any time in Harrisonburg, Mr. Rockleford?"

"Nope," he answered. "I dropped Ms. Williams off at the Harrisonburg exit ramp and got right back on the highway afterward. I didn't even go into the town."

"And you say that you were back here in Midville at 5:20, the time the bank robbery took place in Harrisonburg?" asked the Chief.

"Yesiree," said Rockleford confidently. "Look, I'm a reformed bank robber, not an active one. I have no desire to rob banks anymore."

"I don't suppose there's anyone here in Midville who can verify that you were here when the robbery was committed?" asked the Chief. "In other words, did anyone see you here in Midville at 5:20?"

Rockleford shook his head. "Nope, I went straight home to take a nap."

"Where do you live, Mr. Rockleford?" inquired Cal.

"Right next to the highway's off ramp, here in Midville."

Cal continued writing in his notebook. "So the entire round trip was spent driving on the highway?"

"Yes it was, kid." Rockleford's eyes narrowed. "What's that got to do with anything?"

Cal held up his notebook. "Chief, no one saw Mr. Rockleford in Midville at 5:20 because he wasn't within miles of here," said Cal. "His story simply isn't up to speed. I suggest you book him on suspicion of bank robbery."

How did Cal know that Casey Rockleford was lying about being back in Midville when the crime was committed? *Solution on page 281.*

THE CASE OF THE SEEMINGLY PERFECT ALIBI

The loud roar of machinery made junior detective Cal Q. Leiter and Midville Police Chief Smart cover their ears as they trudged through the Fabulous Fabrics cloth factory. Everywhere they looked, the two friends saw huge mechanical devices that shook and shimmied and banged and clanged.

"Where's the owner's office?" shouted Cal.

The Chief pointed ahead. "Down there," he yelled, his voice almost lost in the ear-splitting noise that filled the building, "near that soda machine."

By the time Cal and Chief Smart reached the office, their ears were ringing. Eager to escape the blare of the thundering machinery, the Chief and Cal pounded on the office door. After a few seconds, the door opened and a lady appeared. Her name tag told Cal and the Chief that she was Ms. Farrington, one of the factory's co-owners. Following introductions, Ms. Farrington led the two detectives into the office.

"Please tell us what's been going on," said the Chief when everybody was seated.

"We've got a thief among us," said Ms. Farrington. "A couple of watches were stolen from some employees' lockers this morning between 8:00 and 9:00."

"Any suspects?" asked the Chief.

"We thought we had one," answered Ms. Farrington. "A man named Lester Hackett. We found the stolen watches in his lunchbox, which he accidentally dropped on his way to the cafeteria. The lunch box broke open and the two watches fell out. "

The Chief looked puzzled. "Why is he no longer considered a suspect?"

"Because he has a reliable person who can provide him an alibi."

"We need to talk to that person," said Chief Smart sternly.

Ms. Farrington frowned. "You have been." She blushed a deep crimson. "I'm his alibi."

The Chief leaned forward. "This I gotta hear."

"Mr. Hackett is a new employee. He works in the cutting room. Today he was working all alone and we had only one machine working, so I went and watched him get started at precisely 8:00."

Cal broke in. "So you were with Mr. Hackett from 8:00 until 9:00?"

"Well, no," she answered. "I left after he got started, but I returned at exactly 9:00 to check in on him."

Again, the Chief looked confused. "How, then, are you his alibi? He had lots of time to leave the cutting room unnoticed."

"Let me explain: Mr. Hackett operates the cloth cutter. The machine does all of the work, but we need an operator to push the a button to get the machine to cut. Anyway, the machine makes one cut per minute. After each cut is completed, the operator pushes the button to start the next cut." She stopped talking and took a deep breath. "Anyway, from 8:00 until 9:00, Mr. Hackett cut a 60-yard piece of cloth into 60 one-yard pieces. That's 60 cuts in 60 minutes. So that means Mr. Hackett could not possibly have left the cutting room during the hour."

"How far are the employee lockers from the cutting room?" asked Cal.

"Just across the hall; you can get there in ten seconds."

The Chief made a sour face. "Cal, where are you going with this?" he said in an impatient voice. "Let's say it takes ten seconds to get there, then twenty or thirty seconds to grab a couple of watches from the lockers, and another ten seconds to return. That's almost one minute. Ms. Farrington said Mr. Hackett had cut sixty one-yard pieces of cloth in sixty minutes. Hackett had absolutely no time—not even a second—to spare."

Cal smiled. "But there's one small aspect of this situation you are not taking into consideration," he said. "Hackett did have time to commit this robbery; I can prove it."

What did Cal figure out that the Chief had missed?
Solution on page 280.

SOLUTIONS

Hit-and-Run Taxi (page 235)

Given the facts, Cal organized the information as follows: Bill on receipt minus driver's initial rate = charge for additional miles.

Freddy's	Smalltown	ASAP
$3.90	$3.90	$3.90
−1.00	−1.10	−.50
$2.90	$2.80	$3.40

So 3.3 miles minus driver's initial rate distance = the miles driven after the initial rate distance:

3.3	3.3	3.3
−.5	−.5	−.2
2.8	2.8	3.1

Since each taxi charged $.10 for each additional .1 mile (a 1 to 1 ratio) after the initial rate part of the ride, the amount charged for the additional part of the trip and the mileage driven for the additional part of the trip will match up for the guilty driver. Therefore, looking at the work above, the numbers show that Smalltown Taxi—Mary Jill Haverhill—was the attacker.

The Chief's Old Partner (page 240)

When Cal did the math, he came upon a huge flaw. Judkins said that he started on the ground floor, which on a vertical number line would be considered zero. (The floors numbered 1 to 15 would be considered positive numbers on the number line, while the basement floor would be considered negative one, −1). When Cal added the numbers that Judkins had written in his tally worksheet, he at one point calculated a −2. That, of course, would be impossible, since the basement (−1) is the lowest floor in this building. Therefore, it proves that Judkins wrote these numbers in without actually having operated the elevator. There are other numbers that were impossible too.

Carnival Probability (page 226)

The probability of tossing three coins and getting two heads is the same as tossing three coins and getting one head. In both cases, the probability is 3 out of 8. Therefore, to make the money aspect of the game fair, it should be $2 to play with a $4 prize ($2 profit), not a $3 prize ($1 profit) when the customer wins. With the dishonest way the vendor has the game set up, he has a sure money-winner of a game for himself.

Mayor's Red Office (page 231)

The least common multiple of 2 and 6 is 6. Together, it took Sue and Harry 2 hours to do one room, so that means that together they could do 3 rooms in 6 hours. Alone, Sue can do one room in 6 hours. Therefore, subtract 3 minus 1 to get 2 and that proves that Harry alone can do two rooms in 6 hours or 1 room in 3 hours. He had enough time to paint the room and drive over to the mayor's place, vandalize her office, and drive back to the hotel by 11:15.

Pizza Decision (page 257)

Answer: A pizza is a circle. To figure out the area of a circle you must square the radius (multiply the radius by itself) and multiply that answer by pi (3.14).

(Remember, a radius is half the size of a diameter.) So the area of a small pizza is $6 \times 6 \times 3.14$ or 113 square inches, while the area of the large pizza is $12 \times 12 \times 3.14$, or 452.16 square inches. Therefore, the area of four small pizzas is found by multiplying 113×4, which equals 452 square inches, the same area as one large pizza. Since four small pizzas cost $22 (4 times $5.50) and one large pizza costs $11, you figure $22 minus $11, or $11 is saved by buying one large instead of 4 small.

Fishy Alibi (page 261)

All three guys left the wharf at 8 A.M. Paddy took 3 hours each round trip, Malcolm took 6 hours, and Frank 4 hours. When you count by threes, fours, and sixes, the lowest number in common is 12. That means 12 hours after they all began, or 8 P.M., is the first time that all three would retun to the wharf at the same time. The only one who was at the wharf at 4 P.M. was Frank. The other two were still out on the water at 4:00 P.M.

Seemingly Perfect Alibi (page 271)

To get 60 pieces, only 59 cuts are necessary. When Hackett made the 59th cut, the result was the second to last piece *and* the last piece with that single cut. So he did have one minute of extra time to steal the watches.

Carpet Dealer (page 247)

Although the Chief's math was correct, Cal's picture proved that Shady Sadee was lying. The combined areas of the five carpets *was* less than the area of the warehouse. But when Cal drew a picture, it was clear that all five of the unrolled, stretched-out carpets could not fit on the warehouse floor without overlapping. (Try this by drawing a picture.)

Missing Country Club Funds (page 253)

When Cal added the five fractions $\frac{1}{4} + \frac{1}{5} + \frac{1}{20} + \frac{1}{18} + \frac{3}{10}$, he got a sum of $\frac{154}{180}$, or $\frac{77}{90}$. Cal realized that the five fractional parts should add up to one whole. That means that $1 - \frac{77}{90}$, or $\frac{13}{90}$ of whatever had been in the treasury fund was missing.

Reformed Bank Robber (page 266)

Mr. Rockleford drove the car exactly at 55 mph on the way to Harrisonburg, and this trip took exactly two hours; the distance of the trip was 110 miles. To leave Harrisonburg at 4:00 and to be back in Midville at 5:20, Mr. Rockleford would have had to drive at about 83 mph (110 miles divided by 1⅓ hours). But this would be impossible, as the mechanic said the car would be lucky to reach 65 mph; therefore, Mr. Rockleford could not have been back home in Midville at 5:20.

INDEX

Illustrations appearing in this book on pages
10, 34–128, 134, and 227–274 are by Lucy Corvino.

Illustrations on pages 16, 20, and 129 are supplied
by Bob Peterson

Illustrations appearing in this book between pages 148–201 are
by Tatjana Mai Wyss

WHAT IS MENSA?

Mensa—The High IQ Society

Mensa is the international society for people with a high IQ. We have more than 100,000 members in over 40 countries worldwide.

The society's aims are:
- To identify and foster human intelligence for the benefit of humanity;
- To encourage research in the nature, characteristics, and uses of intelligence;
- To provide a stimulating intellectual and social environment for its members.

Anyone with an IQ score in the top two percent of the population is eligible to become a member of Mensa—are you the "one in 50" we've been looking for?

Mensa membership offers an excellent range of benefits:
- Networking and social activities nationally and around the world;
- Special Interest Groups (hundreds of chances to pursue your hobbies and interests—from art to zoology!);
- Monthly International Journal, national magazines, and regional newsletters;
- Local meetings—from game challenges to food and drink;
- National and international weekend gatherings and conferences;
- Intellectually stimulating lectures and seminars;
- Access to the worldwide SIGHT network for travelers and hosts.

**For more information about
Mensa International:**

www.mensa.org
Mensa International
15 The Ivories
6–8 Northampton Street
Islington, London N1 2HY
United Kingdom

**For more information about
American Mensa:**

www.us.mensa.org
Telephone: (800) 66-MENSA
American Mensa Ltd.
1229 Corporate Drive West
Arlington, TX 76006-6103 US

**For more information about
British Mensa (UK and Ireland):**

www.mensa.org.uk
Telephone: +44 (0) 1902 772771
E-mail: enquiries@mensa.org.uk
British Mensa Ltd.
St. John's House
St. John's Square
Wolverhampton WV2 4AH
United Kingdom